MW01126742

"With the same narrati settings he demonstrated h̶.̶ ̶.̶.̶.̶ ̶n̶o̶v̶e̶l̶,̶ ̶B̶r̶o̶t̶h̶e̶r̶ ̶S̶l̶e̶e̶p̶e̶r̶ ̶A̶g̶e̶n̶t̶,̶ ̶J̶a̶c̶k̶ *O'Keefe again has crafted an uncompromising, inspirational tale of courage and determination in his latest work, Famine Ghost: The Genocide of the Irish. The period O'Keefe examines is that of the Great Hunger in Ireland, 1845-1850, and his central character, a fearless lad named Johnjoe Kevane, comes to embody the deep spirit and rugged resilience of the Irish people. This is truly a novel that not only remembers but also teaches."*

Jim Kozicki, author of Black Beauty, Owl Light, *and* The Lump

"O'Keefe has delicately balanced history with touching humanity and humor. He has provided readers with a vivid tale, surprising in all the right ways, and an unabashed glimpse into the shocking truth of the Irish Famine. A masterful read cover to cover."

Sara Wolski, literary agent

"Famine Ghost captures the realities of the 1845-1850 Great Irish Famine and is filled with valuable research on the tragedy. An imaginative and thoughtful author, O'Keefe has a real gift for the dialog and pace of language of 19th century Ireland. His vivid portrayal and historical perspective bring the hardships of Ireland's troubles to our awareness in the 21st century, like no other book."

Helen Gallagher, author of Social Media Handbook, Release Your Writing, and Computer Ease

Computer Clarity
www.cclarity.com
SPAWN.org Membership Chair

"The Society of Friends did much to stay the plague and their work was carried on by volunteers who asked no reward. [The Quakers] spent no time in idle commenting on the Protestant or Papist faith, the Radical, Whig, or Tory politics, but looked at things as they were and faithfully recorded what they saw. They relieved, they talked and wrote but acted more. As I followed in their wake through the country the name of "blessed William Forster" was on the lips of the poor cabiners. When the question was put Who feeds you, or who sent you these clothes, the answer was 'the good quakers lady and they that have the religion entirely.'"

Asenath Nicholson

Famine Ghost

Also by Jack O'Keefe, Brother Sleeper Agent: The Plot to Kill F.D.R. Outskirts Press, 2008

Famine Ghost

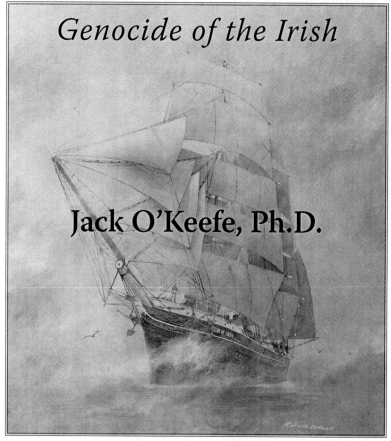

Genocide of the Irish

Jack O'Keefe, Ph.D.

Painting by Richard De Rosset

iUniverse, Inc.
Bloomington

Famine Ghost
Genocide of the Irish

iUniverse books may be ordered through booksellers or by contacting:

iUniverse
1663 Liberty Drive
Bloomington, IN 47403
www.iuniverse.com
1-800-Authors (1-800-288-4677)

ISBN: 978-1-4620-1022-6 (sc)
ISBN: 978-1-4620-1023-3 (ebk)

Printed in the United States of America

iUniverse rev. date: 05/24/2011

This book is dedicated to the memory of the English and Irish Society of Friends (Quakers) who saved hundreds of thousands of Irish lives in The Great Hunger doing what England would not—feed the starving people.

Preface

My introduction to the Irish genocide came not from my old-country mother and father whose own parents had lived through it. My father was born in 1897 in the village of Hospital near Limerick, my Uncle Ed in 1887, yet I never heard one word about the Famine.

After attending Mass one Sunday morning at Old St. Patrick's Church in Chicago, my family and I visited a traveling exhibit on the Famine that had been assembled in the courtyard next to the church. An Irish group promoting knowledge about The Great Hunger brought artifacts, including blow-ups of the records from the British Museum of Irish exports to England during the five terrible years of 1845-1850. Most menacing was a drop-lid coffin made of varnished pine or plywood with a hinge at the bottom for release of the body into the grave. This one coffin dropped members of an entire village into their graves.

The display piqued my interest, especially since I had not heard of the Famine in our family history, which seemed to go back only to the 1920s and the Black and Tans, the British irregulars the English dredged up to terrorize the Irish while the real soldiers were demobilizing after fighting the Germans in The Great War. With their uniforms of khaki and black, hence black and tans, these troops brought murder and mayhem to the Irish, to the extent that England finally had to withdraw them.

Dragged off to Irish dances at Carpenter's Hall on Chicago's south side, my brother and I stuffed ourselves with hot dogs and soda pop and listened to fiery speeches from my uncles about the Easter Rising and the evils of the Tans. We learned no history before that, perhaps because those events of the Rising were more recent, more than sixty years after the Famine, and the war with England spoke of Irish bravery. My mother never told us of her childhood in Ballyristeen, a town land outside Dingle. My mother kept any skeletons in the family closet locked in there. We kids never heard them. My general sense is that the grinding poverty that drove my mother and aunts to America to work as cleaning ladies and my two uncles to England to labor in the steel mills was so much to bear, that my mother had to be coaxed into returning to Ireland for a visit in 1969.

As kids, my brother Dennis and I had to cart in our red "Radio Flyer" wagon what we called "care packages" for my Irish cousins to the post office on Cottage Grove at Easter and Christmas—with money sewn inside the labels of clothes and once a canned ham. On visiting Ireland with both my parents in 1969, I was shocked to find my Dingle cousin Tommy wearing my brown graduation suit from high school ten years earlier, part of a care package.

Because my mother was from Kerry where Mother England had been unable to extirpate the Irish language (not for want of trying), she lapsed into her native tongue on the phone when discussing with her sisters, my aunts, the failings of my brother and me or when talking of family secrets. Robert Scally has a wonderful book: *The End of Hidden Ireland* in which he explores the effects in one townland of The Great Hunger. Even in my own family, a hidden Ireland lived. In 1994 twelve years after my father's death, I learned from a cousin in Ireland that in 1921 as a young man my dad was an IRA soldier who took part in the arrest and execution of an informer to the Black and Tans searching for IRA leader Liam Lynch. My father also helped burn down the British barracks in Kilmallock. Wanted by the English, my father had to flee the country. Neither my brother nor I had heard of this, perhaps not even my mother.

Small wonder then that the Famine was "hidden." The historian O'Grada explains, "people would be glad if the Famine were forgotten so that the cruel doings of their forebears would not be again renewed and talked about by neighbors." And again "echoes of half-forgotten conflicts probably persisted until recently, subconscious or half-forgotten. Ignoring the guilt and the shame leaves the way open in due course for a version of Famine history in which the descendants of those who survived all became vicarious victims." O'Grada goes on to say that "all the information you'd get from the old people was their graves are there (they died in the year of disaster) [1847], while in Ballymoe, County Galway, those who had witnessed the horrors of the famine were reluctant to give details, and only an occasional incident was handed down."

This view of hidden Ireland stands in sharp contrast to what others say of Irish folk history. De Tocqueville points to "a terrible exactitude of memory among the Irish peasantry. The great persecutions are not forgotten." And this is my sense. We Irish don't forget.

* * *

Famine Ghost is a work of literary fiction; the history is true, the plot and characters serving as a framework for telling of The Great Hunger. I have used eyewitness accounts such as Whyte's *Famine Ship Diary*, Nicholson's *Annals*, De Vere's account of life aboard a Famine ship, and quotations from English leaders Trevelyan, Russell, and others. British newspapers like *The London Times* and *Illustrated London News* provide the British side of things while Irish papers, *The Nation* and *The Freeman's Journal* the Irish point of view. Much of the material about the Quakers I have gleaned from Hatton's invaluable *The Largest Amount of Good*.

It's difficult to write a book about an event that was both complicated and depressing, like writing about the Holocaust, but heroes abounded, chiefly the Quakers, many of whom worked themselves to death for the starving Irish. Asenath Nicholson, American widow and philanthropist, is another, as well as many Anglican and Catholic priests, the Sisters of Mercy, the Christian Brothers, and the Dominican Fathers.

Though no exact figures on either mortality or emigration exist, we know that Ireland had a pre-Famine population of eight million. According to a modern scholar, Norita Fleming, "it is commonly accepted that from Ireland to Grosse Ile, in the ocean graveyard, bodies could form a continuous chain of burial crosses." By 1911 Ireland's population was four million, half of the number before the potato blight and the emigrations.

Those interested in more scholarly works may consult the Conclusion, the Epilogue, and the Bibliography. My purpose has been to tell the story of the Famine to draw the reader's interest in much the same way as the drop-lid coffin and other exhibits moved me in Old St. Patrick's many years ago. In the end, only the individual reader can judge whether or not I have succeeded.

Acknowledgments

For help with my writing, I'm grateful to Jerry Palms, Pat Thomas, Gordon Mennenga, Jim Kozicki, Brooke Bergan, Cate Wallace, Lisa Rosenthal, Pat Brixie, Brian and Pat Shanley, Cheri Lynn, Helen Gallagher, Jim Faranda, Sara Wolski, John Winters, Jim O'Connor, Maureen Connolly, Christine Forbes, Brother Ron Lasik and Brother Dan Crimmins, Mary Wersells, Kevin Haggerty, Dr. Ed Finegan, Dr. Jim Valek, and Chris McKenna.

For computer help thanks to Srunyoo Buranavanit of sburanav@ yahoo.com. I am indebted to Steve Taylor for allowing me to use his website of Famine sketches and drawings—Views of the Famine at http://adminstaff.vassar.edu/sttaylor/FAMINE/.

Thanks to my family for putting up with me: Phyllis, Jack and Becky, Kevin, Denis and Terese.

To Jim with Thanks,

Jack O'Keefe

Chapter 1

THE EJECTMENT.

"The fearful system of wholesale ejectment, of which we daily hear, and which we daily behold, is a mockery of the eternal laws of God—a flagrant outrage on the principles of nature. Whole districts are cleared. Not a roof-tree is to be seen where the happy cottage of the labourer or the snug homestead of the farmer at no distant day cheered the landscape."

Illustrated London News, December 16, 1848

From Steve Taylor Website Views of the Famine

http://adminstaff.vassar.edu/sttaylor/FAMINE/

From his parents' cottage, Johnjoe Kevane saw them come with the dawn, the fog drifting up from Dingle Bay a mile away and clinging to Conor Pass above. Six mounted dragoons, wearing their scarlet short-tailed jackets in service to the Crown, rode up to the Kevane cottage in Ballyristeen, two miles north of Dingle, which jutted out into the Atlantic like a large bumpy finger. Each soldier carried across his shoulders a bayonet-fitted musket called a "dragon" because it "breathed fire" when shot. Captain Patrick Packenham with his five soldiers was to preside over the destruction of another farmer's cottage.

Trailing the soldiers like stray puppies this day was Bailiff Sheedy, the landlord's "gombeen man" or rent collector, who preyed upon the poor. The bailiff had conscripted two townspeople, "Irish destructives," the villagers called them. Armed with crowbars and sledgehammers, they wouldn't look the Kevanes in the eye. They would do the dirty work, and looked the part, dressed in patched farmer's clothes, a contrast to the spit and polish of the English dragoons whom they knew despised them for their poverty.

The bailiff strode to the door of the thatched whitewashed cottage and pounded on it with his fist. "Now, John, Mary, 'tis time. I warned ye." Two days before, the bailiff had told John Kevane: "What the devil do we care about you or your black potatoes. It was not us that made them black. You will get two days to pay the rent, and if you don't, you know the consequences." This morning the consequences were arriving.

A weeping woman with ebony hair opened the door, dragging her husband John and holding the hand of her son Johnjoe, a youth with none of the reticence adolescent boys display. "Please, Bailiff, I've been packing all night. Just a few minutes to gather our things, like."

"All right so, but hurry on. Captain Packenham hasn't got all day to waste on the likes of ye. We must tumble more houses." This was said more to impress the captain than to expedite the tearing down of the home. Bailiff Sheedy was afraid of the soldier whose service in the Light Dragoons was marked by his golden sash of captain, the silver Victoria's battle cross he fingered on his chest, and a black patch covering the empty socket of the left eye that he had lost in his battle with the Punjab. Every time Sheedy talked with the officer, he tried to avoid looking at that patch, but it never worked. He could see only the patch, the patch, the patch. Like the Victoria medal on his chest, the captain had earned the patch.

The boy's dog, a brown and white border collie, guarded a few sheep huddled together near the house. From the moment the soldiers arrived, the dog had not ceased barking. The dragoons remained on their mounts, impassive to the destruction of another Irishman's hovel. They kept their thoughts to themselves.

Johnjoe led the family from their cottage. They carried their clothes, a frying pan and a kettle wrapped in blankets, and a wooden crucifix poking out from one corner of a blue woolen quilt. For a moment the father considered rushing the bailiff, but his son held him by his arm. "No trouble now, Da. We agreed."

"May God smite ye all," the father shouted, taking in the bailiff and his men and the haughty dragoons in a sweeping motion of his arm. "Destroying the little we have, sure, you're hell's army."

Two red spots of anger appeared high on the captain's cheeks, and Lieutenant Benjamin Thomas knew it would take little more for their leader to smash his bright Indian sword—the *kirpan*— on the man's head, the same weapon that had cut out his eye. Thomas prayed that the farmer would go quietly, and he shuddered, recalling the "pitch capping" of a stubborn farmer in neighboring Ballyferriter, the captain pouring hot tar in a conical cap on the victim's head, lighting it, and then tearing it off the man's head, ripping away pieces of his face and skull, leaving the farmer mangled and crazy. The lieutenant also remembered another man in Anascaul where the captain employed "half-hanging," a rope pulled tightly around the man's neck until he became unconscious. The captain threw a bucket of cold water over the victim to revive him and repeated the procedure until the farmer expired. Thomas wondered at his

3

captain's cruelty, that a man who had suffered so much could inflict such pain on others. It may have been that lashing out at the rest of the world could somehow allay his own torment.

"Hush, now, love," said John's wife, she and her son holding the father's arms, clinging to him to save his life.

The bailiff jostled Mrs. Kevane as he headed for the cottage door, triggering a leap at him from the sheepdog. Using his bayonet like a spear, Captain Packenham impaled the brown and white mass of fur in mid air. The dog howled and spurted blood.

"For God's sake, man, end the poor creature's misery," screamed Johnjoe.

"As you wish," the captain replied, and cut the dog in two with his kirpan.

"You're expert in destruction and death, you are, the devil's own," shouted John Kevane as his wife threw her arms about him and pulled him off to the side. "Sure, 'tis no wonder someone took out your eye.'"

The captain wiped his bloody saber on the side of his shining black boot and sat unmoving on his gray horse, except for the twitching of his black eye patch, the tic a sure sign of the anger bubbling within. Disentangling himself from his parents, Johnjoe brushed aside the bailiff and strode right to his collie bleeding in a pile at the feet of the captain's horse. He looked straight in the captain's face and then bent down to pick up the dismembered body of his dog. As the boy did so, Lieutenant Thomas begged God that his captain not smash his sword down on the youth. The horse recoiled a step or two, perhaps at the smell of blood. Johnjoe reverently picked up the still-quivering remains of his dog and deposited them in the soft grass near the cottage where he would bury them later.

After the tension of the dog's grisly end, the wreckers proceeded with their work. One of the bailiff's men rushed into the house with two unlit torches. Using the fire from the hearth, the man set the torches ablaze and returned outside. The second destructive seized one of the firebrands and dashed to the back of the house. The two men hurled the flaming wood onto the thatched roof, which burned quickly.

Clinging desperately to each other in their grief, John, Mary, and Johnjoe watched their house burn down, their meager furnishings with it. The blaze devoured the table where they had eaten their meals, the chairs, and the two beds. Smoke and soot covered the family. When the fire cooled after two hours, the bailiff and his men attacked the walls, now blackened with ashes. They brought the walls down with sledgehammers and used ropes to tear down any pieces of the whitewashed stone left standing.

Throughout the long morning, the Kevanes stood huddled together and silent until the end, not one stone of their home left standing on another.

During all this time Lieutenant Thomas focused his attention on the young boy, perhaps sixteen. Though he joined his mother in holding onto John Kevane, the brown-haired youth stood tall and unafraid after picking up his dog, taking everything in, as though wishing to memorize every detail. On the cusp of adulthood, this boy would some day grow into a man to be reckoned with. The lieutenant could see it in his eyes. He didn't think he would have shown the same courage as the boy had in retrieving the mutilated body of his dog at the captain's feet.

"Off to the workhouse with ye, now. You can either live there or get your tickets for Canada," the bailiff said. "A chance for a new life thanks to the generosity of your landlord Major Mahon."

Dazed, the Kevanes trudged through Dingle to the workhouse, a journey many of their neighbors had already made. They sold their few sheep to a friend and carried their belongings in blankets. The dragoons ambled back to the road, their sabers shining in the sun of a new day, their scarlet uniforms out of place with the blackened ruins they left behind. The bailiff and his minions followed, about to reenact the same scene at Aherne's up the mountain.

As they rode off, Lieutenant Thomas knew his captain still smarted from the peasant's remark about his lost eye. The year before in Northern India, Captain Packenham had bayoneted the brown bastard who marked him forever and shot him for good measure. The dragoons had won the Battle of Modkree for the British East India Company and annexed the Punjab, comprising the two provinces of Lahore and Multan. But the captain had left his eye there. The lieutenant realized that John Kevane would never know how close that day he came to death.

IRISH EMIGRANTS LEAVING HOME.—THE PRIEST'S BLESSING.

" . . . I came to a sharp turn in the road, in view of that for which we sought, and of which I send you a sketch, namely, the packing and making ready of, I may say, an entire village—for there were not more than half-a-dozen houses on the spot, and all their former inmates were preparing to leave. Immediately that my rev. friend was recognised, the people gathered about him in the most affectionate manner. . . . He stood for awhile surrounded by the old and the young, the strong and the infirm, on bended knees, and he turned his moistened eyes towards heaven, and asked the blessing of the Almighty upon the wanderers during their long and weary journey."

Illustrated London News, May 10, 1851

http://adminstaff.vassar.edu/sttaylor/FAMINE/

When they reached the high wooden doors of the workhouse, a long rectangular building of two stories, the Kevanes pounded loudly. A worker pulled open a heavy iron bolt, and they walked in. Once inside, they went through an open courtyard where men sat on the ground smashing stones with hammers, useless toil, for ten hours a day, six days a week. The men all wore gray uniforms like convicts. One of their former neighbors, Michael Manning, called out to John Kevane: "John, it's sorry I am to see you in here. Welcome to hell."

The Kevanes entered the stone building, which smelled of damp and rot. The master of the workhouse, Richard Daley, a stocky little man, interrogated the Kevanes, making them stand in front of him while he sat in a chair in a large dimly-lit room like a judge about to pass sentence on the condemned. "You know you've got to prove you're poor."

"Go and look at the smoking ruins of our cottage," John Kevane replied. "And you'll get a bellyful of proof."

"So, Kevane, I suppose someone sent ye."

"Bailiff Sheedy from the estate of Major Mahon."

"Take off those rags you're wearing and be quick about it. A pile of stones is waiting for you and your son to smash outside. We'll have to wash and fumigate you. The dormitory for the men is to the left, women to the right. No talking during meals, and ye can get together as a family only on Sunday for church. No bad language, no disobedience, no laziness, and no family reunions. Families who gather together are punished by flogging or being placed in solitary confinement."

Shoving some papers at John Kevane, Daley growled, "Here. Sign these."

"Not so fast, Mr. Daley. We'll have a look around first."

Daley muttered but the Kevanes departed to inspect the place.

Mary Kevane went over to talk to some women whom she knew from Dingle town. They were knitting in a dark room heated by a small fire, yarn and thread piled on tables. "Mary, if ye have a choice, don't stay here," said Delia Slattery. "Sure this is only a prison with another name."

Johnjoe met a friend from school, Richard Rowe, who brought him to the door of the sick room: "Mind you don't go in, Johnjoe. These people are not long for this world." Inside were eight people on cots, men and women of middle age and older, fighting for breath. In the room was one wide window, partly open. "The wooden planks leaning down to the outside slide the dead bodies down easier to the pit where they're covered with quicklime and dirt," Richard said. "Sure they've run out of coffins."

Johnjoe summoned his mother and father and brought them to the room. Eight people were dying. That was enough for John Kevane who marched the three of them back to Daley.

"We'll not be staying here, Mr. Daley. This is a house of death. Write us out a ticket for passage to Canada."

Grumbling, the master wrote them out tickets for the *Ajax,* leaving in a week for Canada from Dublin.

As they left the workhouse, they met Michael Manning again. "Not staying, I see. A wise move. If we didn't have so many little ones, I'd be doing the same."

* * *

The trip to Dublin was over two hundred miles, most of which they had to walk except when a kind farmer gave them a ride on his cart. The Kevanes passed several other workhouses, all built on the same model with forbidding stonewalls and a heavy wooden gate. Near the Limerick workhouse, John Kevane said to his wife and son, "These are death traps. Not only is it a humiliation to live there, the fever spreads from one to another being so packed together."

Hundreds of people thronged the roads, in different stages of starvation and sickness. Some died on the roadside. Others lay dead in the fields, dogs devouring the bodies. Still others built "scalps" or "scalpins," holes dug under tumbled cottages with coverings of straw and branches. When the sheriff or dragoons came upon these miserable dwellings, they destroyed them, wanting to drive the evictees to seek the workhouse or passage across the ocean to Canada. The pervasive mood of the people was despair. Never before had the potato blight struck even two years in a row. This time the disaster lasted five years, giving the Irish no time to recover. Beggars were everywhere. Those with children the Kevanes gave a few shillings. The Kevanes came across "fever huts," cottages where the dead rotted inside.

HARRINGTON'S HUT.

"I started for Ballidichob, and learned upon the road that we should come to a hut or cabin in the parish of Aghadoe, on the property of Mr. Long, where four people had lain dead for six days; and, upon arriving at the hut, the abode of Tim Harrington, we found this to be true."

Illustrated London News, February 13, 1847.

From Steve Taylor Website Views of the Famine

http://adminstaff.vassar.edu/sttaylor/FAMINE/

Chapter 2

Prime Minister of England Robert Peel stated the reports of starvation and death in Ireland were exaggerated. A reporter for *The New York Times* in 1846 put the lie to Peel's charges that Famine horrors were overblown:

"Across in a field a death-white corpse is being flung into a mass grave—his skin stretched over protruding bones. I note this horrifying image in my note book. I ask myself why is this tragedy passing unnoticed to the outside world? Where is the help? Two miles onwards I enter a cottage or, more so, a glorified hovel. On entering, the overpowering stench of death and fever fills my nostrils and leaves a sickening sense in my stomach. A smouldering fire is in the hearth. Over in the corner a mother clutches to her child. Her eyes are red from crying. She does not know our presence in the cottage. I go over and, to my horror, find that the child is dead. This I now realize the mother knows and clutches to her baby. The baby is obviously dead for a couple of days. I flee from the cottage—the image of the dead child being intolerable to look at. I walk briskly back to my carriage and tell my driver to drive as fast as he can to the ship departing for America. I cannot wait in this death-filled country a minute longer."

Published in the Irish journal Muintir Acla.

A year after the destruction of the Kevanes' cottage, Major Mahon, the largest landowner in the area, spurred his white gelding toward his estate, anxious for the glass of hot buttered rum that awaited him at home. He had stormed out of a meeting at the workhouse in Dingle where he served on the board of directors with the Quakers and Canon Long. That interfering priest had harangued him the whole time. "You're driving the poor from their land just to graze more sheep," the cleric had shouted. "People for sheep. It's not just."

"It's my land," the Major yelled back. "They haven't given me a shilling in rent for over two years. And I've paid four pounds each for them to go to Canada, money I had to borrow."

"Yes," the demented priest screamed, "but for a few pounds more you could have sent them on safer, faster American ships to New York. Your English masters allow ten square feet per person aboard ship; the American ships, fourteen."

The major was correct. He had paid thousands of pounds for three thousand emigrants to Canada. Almost half of them of them died on the ocean, buried at sea without even a priest's blessing, or within six months of arrival. His tenants who refused to go, he evicted—six hundred families.

In truth, Major Mahon was one of the more benign landlords. The year before he had told a doctor friend, "By giving a little of our time, we shall do much good." But Mahon fell into arrears, and he had to recoup his losses.

All during the meeting at the workhouse, The Society of Friends, do-gooders, had listened to the priest's diatribe and said no word in Mahon's defense. When he approached Garfinney Bridge, the major slowed his horse to prevent damaging its hooves on the rough stone surface. Squinting into the growing dusk leaving its last light on Conor Pass above Dingle Bay, he saw someone with a rifle standing in the middle of the bridge, a ghost of a boy. "Who's that, then?" the Major asked the apparition, the musket shaking as the boy aimed it at the man he had seen only once before inspecting their fields with the bailiff.

"Johnjoe Kevane. I've come 3,000 miles from Grosse Ile and the coffin ship you put us on. You murdered my family."

"I did not. Your family robbed me of my rent, you scut," the Major roared, spurring his horse to run the boy down and slash his face with his riding crop.

The boy's musket burst into life, the sound echoing from the Kerry hills around them, the ball thudding into the Major's chest, all but catapulting him from his crazed mount. The long black boot of his right leg stuck in the leather and iron stirrup and tied him to the gelding, which lurched wild-eyed past the boy onto the bridge, bludgeoning its inert load again and again off the stones.

Not another soul was about, but the horse would soon tire of dragging the body and nibble at the grass by the side of the road where no one would find it until the following morning. The boy debated whether or not to chase the horse down, untangle the body, and bury it in some field. He worried that dogs would eat and mutilate the corpse, but he wanted no more to do with the major. He had no shovel to bury the man, and night was coming on. Besides, he was exhausted.

Starving, he had begun the day stumbling through Dingle after walking thirty miles from Tralee, and reading the placard announcing the meeting at the workhouse. The boy had guessed that the major would attend and make his way home from there. He had then walked the two miles to the pile of blackened stone that was once his home before Bailiff Sheedy and the dragoons tore it down a year earlier, and retrieved the musket covered with straw and canvas from under a cairn of stones at the end of the sheepfold, carefully hidden the previous year by his father when all the trouble began. Johnjoe remembered his father training him to shoot the musket at hare and wildfowl, to fire low and adjust to the kickback. For a moment he stopped at the mound of grass where he had buried his dog, his companion chasing the sheep up and down the hills. The major had stripped him of his childhood.

The boy's rage was spent after shooting the major. He had crossed the Atlantic twice to get his revenge. Now he felt only a sad resignation about what he had done. He gave no thought to his own survival, heedless of whether he would live or die. He supposed he could find a scalpin covered with straw from one of the abandoned houses, and last a few days there. But he had to eat, his mind recoiling at the memory of the starving children on the roads, their faces green from eating grass, and of people lying dead in a ditch along the road where dogs feasted on their flesh. Some victims were buried in fields, with only a sheet and straw to cover them.

Too tired to walk back to the pile of blackened and broken walls that had been his home, Johnjoe would hide the gun close by. He picked his way down the bank below the bridge, and he placed the musket covered with canvas under a pile of rocks. Ravenous, he made his way down Spa Road to the monastery of the Christian Brothers, still careful not to be seen by any townspeople who might know him. Perhaps he could beg a meal from his old teachers.

After sneaking through the darkened town, Johnjoe knocked on the door of the brothers' monastery next to St. Mary's Church on John Street, both buildings made of gray stone. Brother Leonard Keating, his favorite teacher, answered, a brick of a man with dark hair who had never needed a strap to discipline him in class. Holding a candle to Johnjoe's face, he asked, "Who's this then?"

The young man hurled himself into the folds of the brother's black habit. "Brother, they dumped me Ma and Da into a mass grave in Canada."

"Good Lord, Johnjoe, you look like a very skeleton. Come in; come in for a meal and a place to stay. We'll get you a wash and some clothes. You went to Canada and came back."

"Yes, Brother. Me Ma and Da died of the ship fever. Later because of the kindness of Father Moylan, I caught on as a worker with the *Jeanie Johnston*, a timber ship." The boy's tears cut sharp rivulets down his dirty cheeks.

"Well, first, let's get some food into you. Your story can wait."

Brother Leonard led the boy into the monastery kitchen where

13

a shiny, copper-colored cauldron lay atop a low fire. In this the third year of the Great Famine, 1847, the brothers had converted their school of eight classrooms into a soup kitchen and dormitory for starving families evicted from their homes and for whom the workhouse had no space.

"I wish I had more for you than this stirabout, Indian cornmeal, brought by the Quakers from America that we use as a thick soup or porridge. Stirabout has become the national food of Ireland during the Famine."

The boy bolted down his meal, slowing down only with a second helping. They sat in the darkened kitchen, the only light from a candle and the flames under the simmering stirabout. Brother Leonard said, "Your clothes smell musty. I'll put them in the shed across the yard where I have a tub of water and some soap. I'll burn those rags, and fetch you some clean clothes. When you've finished, we'll have a cup of tea and put you to bed."

The boy returned to the kitchen wearing rough brown pants and a heavy blue shirt and carrying a bound book of black leather. Brother Leonard said, "Well, a new man—almost. What's the book?"

"My diary. A journalist on the *Ajax*, Mr. Whyte, showed me how to keep a record of our suffering aboard a coffin ship. He told me to make this my mission, telling the world the story of our voyage."

Johnjoe passed over his diary, scuffed by use and being carried about. The brother glanced at the book and handed it back.

"You can tell the story of our people. A grand idea entirely."

"Brother, I must warn you that I have done something so terrible that you will wish to be rid of me. I'll be a danger to you."

"Get away out of that. You could do nothing so awful. You're a fine young man surviving our national tragedy. You've just made your way back over the sea to where you were born and raised."

Telling his story sparked fresh tears. "Brother, I've done a frightful thing. I shot and killed Major Mahon. They'll find his body on the road tomorrow."

Brother Leonard recoiled in shock, "Good God, lad, the dragoons will hang you."

"I owed it to my parents. The musket ball forced him off his horse with only his leg entangled in the stirrup."

Brother Leonard looked around the room as if seeking guidance from the darkness. He knew that dragoon justice was brutal and that capture meant death.

He turned back to Johnjoe. "Where did you get the gun?"

"An old musket me Da showed me how to use, buried under some stones in the sheepfold. I dug it up to kill the landlord."

Worried about his charge, Brother Leonard sought more details of the shooting. "I hope nobody saw you."

"I don't think so. I caught the Major at the foot of the bridge, coming home from his meeting at the workhouse. When I shouted at him, he charged me on his horse and was going to smash me with his riding crop. I shot him full in the chest."

"I hope you hid the gun."

"Under some rocks near the base of the bridge, hard to find unless you know where to look."

"I suppose there was some mark on it to show it was your Da's."

"His initials carved on the stock, 'J K.'"

"Johnjoe, once you get a few hours sleep, we'll go back for the gun tonight. If the bailiff or the dragoons find it, it will make you a suspect. I can hide it under my habit and shut it away in our attic. It won't be the first one I've put there."

"Brother, what a terrible sin. I was in two minds whether to shoot or not. Then the man drove at me."

"Johnjoe, you're exhausted. Get some rest for now, and we'll talk later. To ease your mind, I can understand why you did the deed. Also, it was self defense when the man charged you. Only God can know our hearts, and He's a merciful judge."

"Thanks, Brother, that's a relief to me. What a heavy thing it is to kill a man, even a bad one."

"Yes."

Brother Leonard took Johnjoe to a corner room of the monastery with a bed of clean straw and a blanket. "I want to keep you out of sight of the others, Johnjoe, because your return will throw suspicion on you, like. I'll close the door. No one will bother you."

"Thanks, Brother."

Johnjoe fell into an agitated sleep. He dreamt of the major's huge white horse charging at him, the whip about to slash his face, and the roar of the gun. When the boy awoke, he recorded as much of the shooting as he could remember in his diary.

Brother Leonard was so shaken he couldn't sleep. Later that night, he roused the boy gently. They walked northeast on the cobbled Spa Road towards the bridge, not a soul stirring, only dogs yelping. Brother Leonard had an oil lantern covered with a canvas hood. As they approached the foot of the bridge, Johnjoe began to shiver and shake revisiting the scene of the shooting. "Don't worry, now, lad. It's almost over," Brother Leonard said, patting the boy's shoulder. They used the lantern under the base of the bridge where the boy had buried the gun. After rooting under a pile of rocks, Johnjoe dug up the musket and handed it, still wrapped in canvas, to Brother Leonard.

"Good God, it's heavy, it is."

Brother Leonard took the musket and hid it under the folds of his black habit. As they walked back through town, the dogs renewed their barking. A cottage door opened and a hulk of a man stumbled out into the lane.

Coming closer, Bailiff Sheedy recognized Brother Leonard. "By the Mass, Brother, it's late for you to be walking about," the man slurring his words because of drink.

"Yes, Bailiff, the boy here from the monastery and I were out praying our beads," said Brother Leonard holding up his rosary with one hand while pressing the gun under his habit against his body with the other.

Squinting in the darkness, Bailiff Sheedy couldn't make out the boy's face. "Come closer so I can have a better look at you."

Johnjoe moved only a few steps nearer.

"Well, Brother, get home with ye. These are not times for walking about, beads or no."

"You're right, Bailiff, thanks. Good night to you."

The two continued on their way. "He was with them when they tumbled our house," Johnjoe whispered to the brother when they were a safe distance away.

"Yes, thank God he's had a belly full of porter, so he didn't examine you closely."

"Brother, I've brought such a burden to you."

"Not a bit of it. You're one of our own. I've taught you and know your Ma and Da. Jesus taught us to reach out to those in need."

"Brother, I need confession. That man's death weighs on me, as evil as he was. He murdered my family, but I took revenge into my own hands."

"Yes. Tomorrow we'll go early to Canon Long's to fetch his horse and buggy, which has room for the two of us. I'll drive you to our school in Tralee. The canon can hear your confession before we leave."

After a few hours of fitful sleep, Brother Leonard went to get the boy up, but found him already awake, tears in his eyes, writing in his diary. "Brother, I had the same nightmare as last night. I shot Major Mahon again."

"What's done is done. The Lord forgives us all, no matter how heavy the sin. The nightmare is the events of the past few days playing themselves out in your mind."

They breakfasted on bread and tea. Brother Leonard gave Johnjoe a floppy black hat to pull down over his face as they walked through the empty town. In the pre-dawn darkness they headed down John Street past the Gothic church to the rectory. Canon Long, a tall, gangling man with gray hair, answered the door. "Sure, Brother

Leonard, it's early you're coming for the horse. I've watered and fed him for you." Peering into the darkness, the priest said, "Johnjoe Kevane, you look like a very ghost. I thought Mahon sent you and your family off to Canada."

The boy nodded.

Brother Leonard spoke up. "He needs confession, Father."

"I can't see what's so important to confess at this awful hour of the morning, but come in."

The priest ushered the boy into a small sitting room with a large crucifix on the wall and a wooden kneeler next to an armchair, a peat fire burning in the hearth. Johnjoe knelt down while the priest wrapped his purple confessional stole around his neck. "Now begin, why don't you, " the priest said.

"Bless me, Father, for I have sinned. It's been a year since my last confession. Oh Father, I shot the major."

"Good God," screamed the priest jumping up from his chair, his sacramental stole falling to the floor.

"I killed him with me Da's gun."

"Good God, lad, what a terrible sin. Sure they'll blame me. The major and I had angry words in the meeting house last night."

Brother Leonard, who had been waiting in the hall, could not help but hear the priest shouting. Coming into the room, he grabbed the priest by the shoulders and tried to settle him down. "Now, Father, look here to me. We have been friends for years, so listen to me. Sure you have witnesses who saw you stay on at the workhouse after the major had ridden off."

"Yes, that's right. The Quakers and the other commissioners. We had tea afterwards. Lad, you're sure you killed him."

"Yes, Father."

"Well, we're well rid of him, (God forgive me) for saying it."

"Canon, this lad's parents died in one of Mahon's coffin ships, while it was in quarantine off Canada. He came back here alone. The major charged at him and tried to run him off the road. Now,

18

collect yourself, Father, and hear his confession. I'll wait in the hall."

"Yes. I took a fright. I'm sorry. I was scared for myself."

The priest then listened to Johnjoe's Act of Contrition, which he said in Irish as he had been taught.

A Dhia, tá doilíos croí orm
gur chuir mé fearg ort,
agus tá fuath fíreannach agam
do mo pheacaí thar gach olc eile,
de bhrí go bhfuil siad míthaitneamhach
i do láthairse,
a Dhia, a thuilleas mo ghrá go hiomlán
mar gheall ar do mhaitheas gan teorainn;
agus tá rún daingean agam,
le cúnamh do naomhghrásta
gan fearg a chur ort arís go brách,
agus mo bheatha a leasú.
Amen.

("God, I am heartily sorry that I made you angry, and I truly hate my sins more than any other evil because they are displeasing in your presence, O God, who deserve my love totally on account of you endless goodness; and I have a firm intention, with the help of your holy grace, not to make you angry ever again, and to amend my life.")

When it was over, the priest blessed the boy saying, "I absolve you of your sins in the name of the Father, Son, and Holy Ghost. For your penance, say one rosary and spend two months doing acts of kindness for the poor and starving among us."

"Thanks, Father."

"Now go in peace, lad, knowing you have the Lord's forgiveness."

When they rejoined Brother Leonard in the hall, the priest was humbled. "I apologize to you both for my outburst. I was wrong. I wish you Godspeed on your journey, Johnjoe. What's told in confession is sacred. It will stay with me until death and beyond."

"Canon," Brother Leonard said, "this has been a shock, like. You're a true priest of the people fighting for us in these terrible times. I'll spirit Johnjoe out of harm's way by saying he's a new postulant for the order whom I'm taking to our seminary in Tralee. Thanks. You're a kind priest."

*　*　*

When the two set out for Tralee, some thirty miles east, dawn had not yet broken. Johnjoe pulled his hat down even further over his face. Brother Leonard said, "Now we'll pass by the major's body and horse on the road, so steel yourself. We'll just say a prayer and keep on going."

Just east of Garfinney Bridge, they came upon the major's gelding foraging for grass by the side of the road, Major Mahon's battered corpse still tied to its stirrup. Unlike Hector, whose body the gods protected from further mutilation from a vengeful Achilles dragging it around the walls of Troy, the major's body was bruised and discolored, dirty from being pulled along the road. No one had discovered the death. Some dogs had begun to nose around the corpse, but they scattered with the approach of the horse and trap. None had eaten it. As Johnjoe began to tremble, he said in Irish. *"Nár aifrí Dia orm é / Go maithe Dia dhom é" (God forgive me.)* Brother, I did this, but he deserved it. He killed hundreds of us." As they continued by, Brother Leonard and the young man said the prayer for the dead, "May God have mercy on his soul, and may perpetual light shine upon him. Amen."

Pink dawn finally began to inch its way over the brown furze of the Slieve Mish Mountains in front of them. To their right the blue and green waters of Dingle Bay raced to the Atlantic.

20

"What a beautiful country to starve in, Johnjoe."

The overflow from the waters running down the mountainside made the road muddy and slick in places, so Brother Leonard guided the horse carefully. As they climbed up Conor Pass, black-lowering clouds descended on them.

When the buggy slipped off on the side of the road, one of the wheels was ready to crack. "Johnjoe, jump off the trap on the side away from the edge. Let me see can I lift the wheel back onto the road. Hold the reins of the horse and pull them toward you when I yell."

Brother Leonard was thick-muscled, but he strained to raise the wheel from the mud so it would stick onto the harder surface of the pass. "Pull the horse to your side now, Johnjoe." Finally the wheel got some purchase on the road, and the trap settled evenly on the path. Sweating heavily, Brother Leonard climbed into the trap. "We'll stop at the nearest lay by for a bit of a rest." His black hair was damp with perspiration.

"'Twas a good job, Brother. Sure, you're strong for a teacher."

"I wasn't always a teacher. Like you, I was raised on a farm where we had to clear the field of boulders. Heaving them round made me thick-muscled."

As they rode along the mountain pass, they saw six evergreens grow in a cluster by the side of the road, enshrouded by a light fog in a gentle rain. Deep valleys plunged down on both sides. At noon they heard horsemen coming up behind them. Six dragoons in their blood-red uniforms halted them.

"Johnjoe, say as little as possible," urged Brother Leonard.

A tall man, Captain Packenham, wearing the golden sash signifying his rank and bearing an eye patch, spoke first:

"Major Mahon is shot dead near Garfinney Bridge, and I'll see his murderer hanged. You did not pass by the bridge."

Brother Leonard felt the youth tremble beside him.

"No, Captain. We came on the road further north."

21

"You must have left Dingle early."

"Captain, I'm driving an applicant to our order, postulants we call them, to our monastery in Tralee."

"You certainly take them young. I imagine you're fifteen."

"Seventeen, Sir," replied Johnjoe.

"Hardly strong enough to hold a musket let alone fire one, but polite I see. Well, proceed. I'm looking for a man who will hang."

The dragoons turned back toward town leaving the two travelers to go on.

"You did well, Johnjoe."

"They were the same men who watched our house tumble, Brother. That captain sliced our sheepdog in two before I could call the poor creature off the fool of a bailiff. Thank God they didn't recognize me."

"Sure, Johnjoe, that was a year ago when they evicted you. They've uprooted so many of our people they can't tell one from the other."

"The thought of an innocent man to die for what I did, Brother. The idea haunts me."

"Perhaps no one will be hanged. "

"I could not live with myself were someone to die for me. But, Brother, I wanted the man dead."

"Look here to me, lad. You confessed your deed to the canon; The Lamb of God washed away your sin with His blood. You believe that."

"Yes."

Chapter 3

BEGGAR-WOMAN AND CHILDREN.

"The Irish beggar-woman! Who that has ever seen or heard ever can forget her? Look at Molly's firstborn. He seems half sad, and yet he's a droll boy, every inch of him."

Illustrated London News, August 12, 1843.

From Steve Taylor's website Views of the Famine

http://adminstaff.vassar.edu/sttaylor/FAMINE/

As the two travelers approached the town of Castlegregory, ten miles from Dingle, they came upon a small abandoned village, Killeton, ivy covering the stone walls, fuchsia, foxglove, and honeysuckle growing where people once lived, the village prey to landlord evictions. Behind the empty town gleamed Brandon Bay on one side, Tralee Bay on the other, ruins engulfed by beauty.

A woman in a faded black dress, holding a baby in her arms and a little boy clutching her skirt approached them. "Please, Father, a coin to buy some bread for these little ones."

Brother Leonard reached into the folds of his habit and found a sovereign to give her as she continued her trek to the workhouse.

"God bless, Father."

"Wait, please, Missus," said Johnjoe and pulled two shillings from his pocket for her.

"God bless," replied the woman.

* * *

Two hours later when Captain Packenham and his men returned to Dingle, the news of the Major's death had spread. The dragoons almost ran down the bailiff, still reeling from a night of drinking. Unshaven and wearing a dirty wool coat, he asked the captain, "I suppose you had no luck in your search."

"No, Bailiff, we met only a priest and a young man riding in a horse and buggy."

"It couldn't have been Canon Long because I just saw him walking on John Street."

"Well, some cleric or other, taking a boy to join the order in Tralee he said."

"Maybe Brother Leonard from the monastery. He might have borrowed the canon's horse and trap. The brothers are too poor to have one."

"Perhaps, Bailiff. The boy with him was seventeen but looked younger, a wraith."

"That's strange, Captain, because late last night I met Brother Leonard and a boy walking from the bridge, saying their beads, like."

"You're thinking this could be the same boy and that he and the clergyman might have had something to do with the major's death."

"It's possible, Captain. They're savages, after all. Those brothers are well in with the people."

"You're right, Bailiff. I'll go back out after them tomorrow. We have to here search first. They would still be miles from Tralee."

Captain Packenham and his subordinate Lieutenant Thomas decided to go to the rectory and speak with Canon Long. The rectory was a small, square farmhouse that sat close to St. Mary's Church.

"Good morning, Captain," the priest said. "Come into the parlor."

"Not a good morning at all. Major Mahon was shot and killed on the road last night."

The three men sat in the small parlor where a fire threw off some heat.

The priest made the sign of the cross and said a brief prayer for the dead. "I'm sorry for his family. Some pay for their foul deeds in this life, some in the next. But I take no joy in his death."

"I'm told the two of you argued at the workhouse last night, and we hear reports that from the pulpit you denounced the major as 'worse than Cromwell.'"

"A damnable lie, that. I said no such thing. Bring the man forward who claims that and let him repeat it to my face. Yes, the major and I quarreled last night. It could not be otherwise, him tearing down the houses of the poor, bringing starvation and death to our people."

"You own a musket, Father."

"I don't. Search the rectory if you like."

"Father, there are those who would wish the major dead."

"Hundreds, Captain. All those poor souls the major drove to the workhouse or onto the roads."

"Bailiff Sheedy tells me you loaned your horse and trap to another clergyman traveling with a young man."

Canon Long said, "Yes, Brother Leonard from the monastery taking a postulant, a new recruit to their seminary in Tralee."

"I suppose you know the boy, Father."

"I can't be sure. Brother Leonard feeds a whole crowd of them at the school, those the workhouse can't accommodate."

"I'm wondering if the clergyman and the boy could be our murderers. The bailiff told me he met them late last night coming home from Garfinney Bridge."

"Captain, I've known Brother Leonard for years. He devotes his whole life to teaching and now providing meals for the poor. He would harm no man. As for the youngster, he would have to get the musket and be strong and skillful enough to fire it."

"That's the question, Father. The boy I met was a stripling, scarcely strong enough to hold the gun. In any case, I'll track them down and question them more closely. I'll find the culprit and hang him. No more inflammatory words from your pulpit, mind."

"Captain, tend to your work of destruction. I'll tend to my pulpit."

As he ushered the two officers out, Canon Long prayed for the safety of his penitent. He hoped that Brother Leonard would get off the road beyond the grasp of Captain Packenham.

For his part, the captain felt Canon Long was not telling all he knew.

* * *

Back at his desk in the barracks, Captain Packenham tried to read his Bible, but he was distracted. He could have let the murderers slip through his hands. And here he was an officer in Her Majesty's Third Light Dragoons reduced to driving peasants from their miserable dwellings in this wretched country. He fingered his service medal proudly, silver with the graven image of Victoria Regina, a blue ribbon underneath. He was the second son of Lord Packenham, a landowner from Roscommon, a "jumper," converting to the Church of England from Catholicism in return for a grant of land from Cromwell, the same way Major Mahon's forebears had acquired their properties. Lord Packenham had left his estate to his eldest son, as was the custom. The youngest had become a minister. From his youth, Patrick prepared for a career in the military, a life for which he was well suited.

Never a student, Patrick had one obsession: he read the Bible avidly. A leather-bound copy of the King James Version, a gift from his dying mother, accompanied him everywhere. Even in Modkree on the edge of the jungle, the book was strapped to his saddlebag. While other soldiers told tales around the campfire, he retreated to his tent to read by candlelight. The other men considered him aloof, but he didn't care. He had his Bible. After being robbed of his one eye in battle, he now read only in daylight to preserve his sight.

In his struggle with his Sikh enemy, he had triumphed, but was marked forever by his conquest. He now saw only half the world because of his wound, his reward a few ounces of silver that hung on his chest and the rounded sword, the kirpan, that had been the instrument of his loss.

Every day he looked in the mirror, he felt again the slash of the blade when he saw the whitened scar that ran from his forehead to his cheek and the gaping hole that had been his eye covered beneath the patch. No one would see the wound but himself. He even slept with the patch. He could have died, perhaps should have died, and would have, except for the ministrations of the surgeon who had sewn his face back together and prevented infection. But his wound was more than physical. The kirpan hacked out his soul as well as his eye with the blow. God preserved him to do his duty. And in this case his duty was clear: to catch and hang the murderer of Major Mahon. Whether it was the young man or the cleric, or both, mattered not. He would have them.

Though Brother Leonard and his charge had survived their encounter with Captain Packenham, they hastened to put more distance between themselves and the dragoons. By late afternoon, the soft rain had stopped, leaving the road muddy. Conor Pass brooded black against a violet sky behind them. Because the road was narrow and steep, Brother Leonard focused on the horse.

"Johnjoe, my people are from Castlegregory, my brother John and his family. I'm thinking we'll get off the road and stay there for the night. We're ten miles from Tralee."

"But we'll be placing them in danger, too. It's enough that I have dragged you into this. I'll have to go off on my own."

"Hush, now, lad. This is my duty as I see it."

"Those dragoons have you worried."

"Yes, the bailiff may have told them of seeing us near Garfinney Bridge last night, throwing suspicion on us, like."

"Brother, I'm an albatross to you, and I need to strike out by myself."

"No more of that. I've prayed over this and chosen to do it."

"Yes, Brother."

More to distract the young man than to obtain information, Brother Leonard said, "Tell me about the voyage across."

"Brother, I'll read what I have in my diary. It's long but will help pass the time."

Chapter 4

SCENE BETWEEN DECKS

"A Scene Between Decks"

Illustrated London News, July 6, 1850

From Steve Taylor's website Views of the Famine

http://adminstaff.vassar.edu/sttaylor/FAMINE/

Johnjoe began reading:

This is the true story of my family, the Kevanes, aboard the ship *Ajax* that sailed from Dublin to Grosse Ile, Canada, during the summer of 1847. I owe much thanks to Robert Whyte, my mentor on ship, who showed me how to keep a diary and allowed me to copy some of his.

May 20

Right at Dublin harbor a doctor, an old man with shaking hands, inspected my Ma, Da, and myself. The man had the smell of The Drink on him. Ma had brought a chamber pot, thank God. 110 of us crowded the ship, many with wee ones. As we pulled away from shore, a farmer from Galway raised his fist at the sky and shouted, "Prime Minister Russell, may you rot in hell forever."

June 2

During the early afternoon, the sky turned black and a storm arose. The waves tossed us up and then down. The roar of the wind was drowned out by a series of thunderclaps. Lightning lit up the black sky. The sailors were about to close the hatches, and I scurried down below to find all in a panic. My Da assured my Ma and me that the storm would pass. It did. But we were sad to discover later Mrs. Murphy dead in her berth. That evening Mr. Whyte, who was writing a diary of our trip, told me that American ships were vastly better than the British. They had more sails and were better navigated. They made eight to ten knots at night. English ships made only half that because they took their sails down at sunset. American shipmasters made better use of the weather. They brought in sails when they saw bad weather approach and raised them again to use the powerful wind that follows a storm.

July 3

After a month at sea, Mr. Whyte, who stayed in a cabin near the captain, not in steerage, said, "Johnjoe, tell me what things are like down below in steerage."

"Terrible, Sir. Below the bottom berth chicken bones, urine, excrement, vomit, and rotten food litter the floor. Everything is covered with maggots. We dare not go about without our shoes on. 'Tis slippery. Even walking is dangerous."

Mr. Whyte told me he was astonished that some passengers had no feeling whatever, either for their fellow creatures' woe with the fever, or in thinking of being themselves overtaken by the dreadful disease.

I replied to him, "Mr. Whyte, that is all we poor people know. In Ireland, the dead are everywhere: on the roads, in ditches, and in the workhouse. We left Famine and death at home only to find it again at sea."

"But, Johnjoe, some don't even mourn their own loved ones."

"You're right, Sir, but on ship we're cut off from our old life. We have no priests to hear our confessions, or say Mass for us. We don't even have a coffin to rest in the cemetery with our ancestors. Only a splash in the water marks our going. We become food for sharks."

"But to show such little emotion."

"Sir, many of them have given up. They have the same blank stare as those you meet on the road going to the workhouse. They're already dead."

Brother Leonard said, "The Lord saved you for a purpose of His own, Johnjoe, like Mr. Whyte, to tell your story to the world. You have your diary to keep matters fresh in your mind."

"Yes, Brother, but the diary also reminds me of the evils Major Mahon inflicted on us."

*   *   *

Before they returned to the road to hunt for Brother Leonard and his companion, Captain Packenham took his men to the brothers' monastery. A tiny man in a black habit and Roman collar too big for his neck answered the door. "I'm Brother Gerald, Captain."

"I'm going to search these premises for the gun that killed Major Mahon."

"This is a house of God, Captain. We have no weapons here."

"We'll see. Stand aside," said the captain, banging the brother against the door.

The troop of six soldiers found fifty people of all ages languishing on blankets and straw in what had been classrooms, long rows of desks and chairs pushed against the walls. Armed with bayonets at the end of their muskets, the men prodded under blankets and bedding. The captain dispatched two soldiers to check the barn while he and the others searched the kitchen and dining room, a small chapel, and the four cells where the brothers slept, each with a cot and chair and wooden crucifix hanging on the wall.

Brother Gerald, a man similar in age to Brother Leonard, trailed the captain and his men. When they had finished, Captain Packenham spoke to him: "We found nothing. I met one of your colleagues on the road with a young man traveling to Tralee."

"Yes, to join our seminary there."

"I imagine you know his name."

"I don't know the youth, Captain. One of the boys staying here."

Packenham was suspicious, certain that this brother was lying to him. Stabbing his finger into the brother's chest, he said, "If they are our murderers, they'll hang."

"I have no fear of that. They're guiltless."

"We'll see. Tomorrow we'll catch up with them on the road."

* * *

Brother Gerald was uneasy about the muskets he had squirreled away in the attic, which the dragoons had overlooked. For some days now he had been repairing the stones of the well near the barn. He first added some bricks with mortar to the top, leaving an opening between the inside and outside walls. When evening fell, he retrieved the three guns from the attic, wrapped them in burlap sacks and straw, and placed them in the space he had made. He used the remaining bricks to top off the well with only a thin layer of mortar. He could easily remove the bricks if it was necessary to retrieve the guns.

That same evening Captain Packenham called on the bailiff, about to launch on another night of porter and ale. "We found no guns at the monastery, Bailiff."

"You checked the attic, Captain. Rumor has it that the brothers hoard guns there for the farmers."

"I saw no attic, but I'll go down and inspect it now."

"Sure, I don't trust those brothers, Captain. As thick as thieves they are. Religious they may be, but they're well in with the people."

The captain with Lieutenant Thomas returned to the monastery and confronted Brother Gerald. "You didn't show us the attic. We'll see it now."

Showing the officers the ladder hidden behind a staircase, Brother Gerald left them to it, one part of him hoping the captain might fall and break his neck. The soldiers found some trunks and desks but no guns.

Early the following morning before they were to give chase to the two travelers, Captain Packenham with his lieutenant in tow decided to have another go at Canon Long. Packenham thumped on the door of the rectory. He was convinced the priest was withholding information.

The priest led them into his parlor where a small fire glowed.

"Canon, you're hiding the name of the young man."

"Sure, dozens of boys crowd the workhouse and the monastery, Captain. I couldn't know them all."

"You've been here a long time, Father."

"Twenty-one years since I came from Kenmare."

"And you would have baptized all Catholic children in that time."

"Yes, Captain."

"I want to see your baptismal registry."

"Of course," said the priest, and brought to the parlor a black leather-bound volume with the names of the baptized and their parents and godparents. The entries were arranged chronologically, the latest just two weeks previous, one of the newer entries. Since the blight began, the birth rate had declined to almost none. The captain ranged back twelve years, looking for boys that age and older. He found eighty-one males between ten and seventeen.

"I'll take your book with me to the workhouse and monastery to check the names."

"Indeed you won't, Captain. That book stays here."

"I assume you've heard of pitch capping," the captain said.

The priest shuddered. Even Lieutenant Thomas recoiled at the mention of this horrible punishment.

"Surely, Captain, you wouldn't torture a poor country priest."

"I will if I don't get the name of that missing boy."

"That book stays here."

Playing the role of mediator, Lieutenant Thomas suggested that the priest cull out the names of the males in question and copy them into a new list. The captain agreed, but warned the priest, "Omit no one, mind. I'll check."

The priest would include Johnjoe among the names, but not mention that the young man had returned to Dingle from Canada.

After the priest wrote down the names, the two officers went to the workhouse which both of them hated, Captain Packenham because it was full of savages, the lieutenant because of the suffering and misery there.

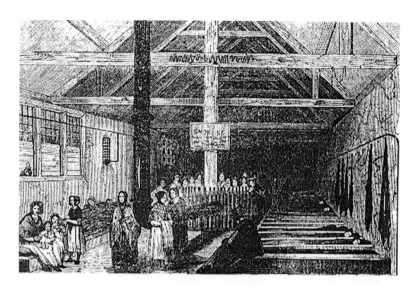

Workhouse interior.

From Steve Taylor's website Views of the Famine

http://adminstaff.vassar.edu/sttaylor/FAMINE/

As the two officers entered the workhouse, they passed a gang of men in an open courtyard smashing rocks with hammers, make-work projects, many of the faces familiar to the two dragoons from tumbling their homes. Inside the two-story building, sixty women of different ages were knitting in a cold, damp room, their goods sold to benefit the workhouse. The matron and two assistants supervised dozens of children in the dining room.

"Good morning, Captain, Lieutenant," said Mr. Daley, a rotund man of middle age, the master of the workhouse, much better fed than his charges.

"We've come to check your register for all young men over twelve years, one of them perhaps the murderer of Major Mahon."

Providing the officers with his own desk and chair, Daley brought them the workhouse log of inmates. Captain Packenham struck twenty names from his list, leaving some sixty still unaccounted for. He would repeat the procedure at the monastery.

On their way from the building, Captain Packenham and Lieutenant Thomas, a few steps behind, passed again the men crushing rocks in the yard.

"Sure 'tis you that destroyed our home and landed us here," shouted a young farmer to the captain. As the man, Michael Manning, raised his hammer, and stumbled towards him, without a moment's hesitation the captain pulled out his revolver and shot him dead. "One less for the workhouse to feed," said the captain to his stunned lieutenant, "and a warning to these others."

Chapter 5

SEARCHING FOR POTATOES IN A STUBBLE FIELD.

"Searching for potatoes is one of the occupations of those who cannot obtain out-door relief. It is gleaning in a potato-field— and how few are left after the potatoes are dug, must be known to every one who has ever seen the field cleared. What the people were digging and hunting for, like dogs after truffles, I could not imagine, till I went into the field, and then I found them patiently turning over the whole ground, in the hopes of finding the few potatoes the owner might have overlooked. Gleaning in a potato-field seems something like shearing hogs, but it is the only means by which the gleaners could hope to get a meal."

Illustrated London News, Dec. 22, 1849

From Steve Taylor's website Views of the Famine

http://adminstaff.vassar.edu/sttaylor/FAMINE/

The two fugitives reached Castlegregory, the village on a neck of land separating Brandon Bay from the Bay of Tralee, the beach here the longest in Ireland.

"Sure, this is a great surprise," said John Keating, a younger version of his brother, the cleric, with hair the color of night as he welcomed the wayfarers into their cottage. The house was whitewashed with a rye-thatched roof, a peat fire burning in the hearth with cane-seated chairs and a rocker around the wooden kitchen table. A picture of the Holy Family, Jesus, Mary, and Joseph with his carpenter's tools hung on one wall; above the beds in a corner, a wooden crucifix. Brother Leonard introduced his sister-in-law Elizabeth, petite with flame red hair, and their fifteen-year-old son Terry to Johnjoe.

"Sure, ye look starved with the hunger, ye do," said Elizabeth as she fried some cockles, potatoes and dulse, the red seaweed picked from the rocks along the shoreline.

"Now, Leonard and Johnjoe, dig in and get something in your stomachs while I make the tea."

After they had eaten and talked, Johnjoe and Terry, two years younger, became fast friends. Like his mother, Terry had red hair and a face dotted with freckles. Bristling with energy, the boy looked as if he might pop through his skin. He talked a mile a minute, hardly giving Johnjoe time to respond. "Johnjoe, we have fine fishing just near here at Lough Gill, wild brown trout. But we have to sneak out early in the morning because the bailiff patrols the shore and levies a fine if he catches us. Mr. Conley was sent to jail for two months because he couldn't pay the fine of thirty shillings. Sure, we can't fish in our own country."

"You're right, Terry. We Catholics can't get licenses to hunt or fish. The English have closed fishing from October 1st to February 12th, more than a third of the year," said Johnjoe.

"Me Da works with the Quaker fishermen here. Thank God we've always food."

38

Telling fish tales, Terry would have talked until dawn, but his mother came to hush him and the young man fell asleep.

With the young men settled for the night, Brother Leonard talked softly to John and Elizabeth. "We're a danger to ye. The dragoons are out hunting for the murderer of Major Mahon."

"But sure neither of ye had a hand in that," replied John.

When his brother remained silent, John realized the seriousness of their visit. He would do anything for his brother, but he had to safeguard his wife and son.

Elizabeth said, "Leonard, we love you, but I'm afraid of the dragoons. They're terrible cruel. They burn down the cottages of any who oppose them, even pitch capping some poor farmers."

"You're my brother, Leonard, and I can tell by the cut of that boy he's a decent young man, no matter what the dragoons may accuse him of. Look how easily he gets on with Terry. Elizabeth is right, but I think we can keep ye a day or two longer. I'll put your horse in a neighbor's field. The buggy I'll hide under some hay in the barn. The dragoons won't come until morning when the two of ye can slip away up to Brandon Mountain and secret yourselves among the rocks."

"John, we're a danger to ye."

Just after dawn the clip clopping of horses filled the silence of the town. The dragoons had caught up with them. Because Castlegregory was on the road to Tralee, the captain wanted to inspect it.

John Keating roused Johnjoe, Brother Leonard already awake.

"The two of ye head up to Brandon Mountain," said John. "No one saw your arrival last night. The village is locked up after sunset. On the climb, stay behind the hedgerows and stonewalls. I'll light a lantern behind our house when it's safe to come down. Mind you be quick."

Running like hunchbacks, the two scaled the hills beyond the house, keeping as low as they could behind the fieldstone walls. Some sheep looked at the strangers curiously. After an hour's hike, they hid among the gray boulders on the mountaintop to peer into the town below. They had to stay still because any movement might attract the attention of the dragoons. Past the village, Tralee Bay gleamed in the distance as the fog began to lift from the water. The red-jacketed soldiers were easy to see as they scuttled from cottage to cottage.

Captain Packenham found the local bailiff, Joseph Murphy, a stocky man in his forties. "We're looking for a religious and a boy riding in a horse and trap in connection with the killing of Major Mahon."

"A priest shot the major."

"Perhaps. They call him 'Brother'. They're supposed to be heading for Tralee. We're going to question some of your villagers, and I want your help."

"Yes, Captain."

In his search, Packenham knocked on the cottage door of widow Muldoon, a woman in her eighties wearing her hair in a tight gray bun. She was petrified of him as she fastened on his eye patch. "Good morning, Ma'am, we're looking for a priest and a young boy riding in a horse and carriage."

"I've not seen them, Sir. Just some dirty tinkers looking to mend some pans. I gave them short shrift. Sure, they'd steal the eye out of your head. Oh, Glory be to God, sorry, Sir."

Both the captain and the old lady blossomed into blushes, the officer always sensitive to his physical loss. He never forgot his affliction, carrying it with him everywhere.

The Keatings were next door. "We've seen no one, Captain," said John.

The captain replied, "We have to search the rest of the town and head for Tralee."

To the Keatings and the watchers on the mountain, it seemed the dragoons would never finish their search. Morning turned into afternoon as the dragoons inspected the church, the rectory, and even the bailiff's house.

"We'll leave it a bit longer to make sure they don't double-back, like," John told Elizabeth.

From their perch high among the boulders of Brandon Mountain, Brother Leonard and Johnjoe watched the scarlet-coated troops ride from house to house until they left the village. "Lad, we came in so late that no one saw us, thank God. Bailiff Sheedy must have put them on to us."

Down below they saw John Keating put a lantern on a boulder in back of their house, so they scrambled down to safety.

Later, when Johnjoe and Terry were asleep, Brother Leonard talked with his brother and sister-in-law. "I'm in a quandary. If we don't show up at the monastery in Tralee, it will be an admission of guilt that we're running from them. But were they to catch us and bring us back to Dingle, it means a noose for the boy. Sure, he's the only one ever to return from a coffin ship."

John said, "The boy has been to Canada and back—a miracle."

"Yes." Leonard said. "A frightful journey. He lost both his parents there."

"Good God, they'll suspect him immediately."

"Yes. I won't see him hang, John."

"I feel terrible sad, Leonard," Elizabeth said, " but we've got to save ourselves from the dragoons. And we have Terry to worry about."

"Sure, I know, Elizabeth. You couldn't have been kinder."

"The captain told me they're off to Tralee," John said. "He is a cold one. I wonder how did he lose his eye."

"Fighting the Punjab in India, poor man, but it hasn't made him any more compassionate to the rest of us," Leonard said.

"Perhaps you could go north to Listowel, bypassing Tralee and then south to Cobh where you might send him away by ship."

"That's what I'm thinking," Leonard said.

Elizabeth said, "I'll bake some bread for your trip."

Long before the morning light, the two fugitives sneaked out of town, wrapping cloth around the horse's hooves to deaden their sound. Only a few dogs barked as they passed, the air around the travelers heavy and damp with fog rising from Tralee Bay below. They first had to take the main road to Camp, passing over the Finglas River and Glanteenassig where a waterfall snaked from the mountaintop through the holly and furze to form Anascaul Lake below.

"Johnjoe, we're going to go around Tralee, where the dragoons will be searching for us at our school. If the dragoons catch us, they'll haul us back to Dingle, and we'd be done for. John and I talked this out, and he agrees with me."

"But, Brother, I'm making you an accomplice, like. Perhaps we should go back to Dingle, and I'll face the charges."

"You will not. I've prayed over this and know we're doing the right thing."

"But you'll be in danger if they catch us."

Brother Leonard knew that Johnjoe was right. By helping his former student, he was putting himself and the order in peril. But the Irish had seen enough of dragoon justice to know that it was a sham. Even if he must sacrifice himself trying to save Johnjoe, he would do it gladly.

As they rode forward, the fog lifted from the Bay of Tralee, revealing an empty road which would get busier the nearer they got to Tralee.

"What I have to say now is hard for you, Johnjoe. Even if I were able to smuggle you into Dublin among our seminary brothers, the dragoons could still hunt you down. You're safer out of the country entirely."

"I won't leave again."

"I know your heart is here, but you don't deserve to die. The brothers in Waterford may know someone who can pay for your passage from Cobh, not far away from them. They'll find a safe, good ship to New York, not a coffin ship."

"I won't go."

"Remember your mission, Johnjoe. You must tell the world what happened to your Ma and Da and why. The landlords, like Major Mahon, must face their accuser—you. You have your diary."

"I won't go, Brother. I'll write my story here."

"Johnjoe, you could be giving away your life. You might be able to take an assumed name and live with the brothers as a novice in Dublin until we can get you away." But even as he said this, Brother Leonard recognized the complications. Novices were free to give up on the seminary during the first year, and any one who left could inform on Johnjoe, exposing him and bringing punishment to him and the order.

"I won't do it, Brother. No one but my Ma and Da have cared for me as much as you. You have placed yourself and the order in danger, even your own family. My past is part of me. I'll tell our story to the world from Ireland or die trying."

Desperate for ways to protect his charge, Leonard said, "But what if we were able to place you among the Quakers who are doing such good work for our people. They have a model farm in Colmanstown, Galway, where we might get you on as a worker-student. You could finish your diary there."

"Brother, I've had a taste of running from the dragoons. I want to be myself, Johnjoe Kevane, and my history is part of me."

"But I want to protect you."

"Yes, Brother, and I'll be thankful till the day I die. But soon I'll have to strike out on my own, both for my sake and yours. You understand, Brother, that I'm grateful, but my life is my own."

"Johnjoe, you'll warn me when you're about to leave."

"Of course, Brother."

One part of Brother Leonard was relieved. The search for

Johnjoe had cast suspicion on Canon Long, the brothers in Dingle and his own brother's family in Castlegregory. He was surprised by Johnjoe's decision and how firmly he was committed to it. Johnjoe was growing into an adult right before his eyes.

As they made their way towards Tralee, beggars crowded the road, even here in the remote passage through the Slieve Mish Mountains covered in some places with reddening furze and others with stones and boulders, as if some Celtic god had lobbed them down from the top of the mountain. The women with children were the saddest, their faces pinched white with hunger, depriving themselves so their children could eat. Brother Leonard and Johnjoe gave away more of their money, a worry to them both because they had so little left. Brother Leonard feared also that every beggar they passed was a potential informer who would bring Captain Packenham down on them.

In the Slieve Mish Mountains, they passed a flattened place where piles of stones were gathered around a single upright stone in the middle, a pagan ogtham stone carved with runic letters, one of 400 scattered about Kerry and West Britain. The road went through spaces carved between two valleys, purple clouds scudding by above them. The hills farther away had a blue tint to them from the mists that crowned them. Even amid such natural beauty, Brother Leonard knew that danger lay ahead. Packenham was like a bloodhound wedded to the chase.

Chapter 6

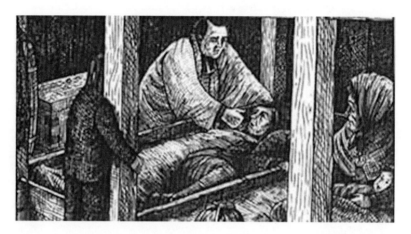

Last rites administered to a dying man aboard a coffin ship at Grosse Ile

Sligo Heritage http://www.sligoheritage.com/archpomano.htm

As they rode east and north through Blennerville and Dromthacker to bypass Tralee, Johnjoe read another excerpt from his diary:

August 1

After ten weeks, we finally reached Grosse Ile, the quarantine station.

This was the day Ma and Da pierced my heart. Me Da said, "Johnjoe, you're the last of us. We've been chased from our home, the place our ancestors lived. If we should die, and death surrounds us, you're to carry on our name."

"Yes, love," Ma said. "Da is right. You're strong, and we love you more than life itself. Mind us and stay away from us if we should catch the fever."

"But, Ma, I can't leave you."

"Johnjoe, you must. We've done our best to stay clean and healthy, but so have others who have died. Johnjoe, you're to take care of yourself—for our sake."

Da became delirious first and his features swelled up. Ma tended to him until she began to feel the headaches herself.

We knew from those who were near us that it was ship fever. Me Ma pushed me out of our berth. She said, "Move away from us now, Johnjoe, and save yourself."

I went on deck to fetch the mistress, saint that she is. When she saw the condition of my parents, she said, "Keep back, lad. You can do nothing for them now."

I hovered nearby while the mistress tended to them. She cleaned their vomit and removed their soiled clothes. She had no fear of catching the illness. I was scared of getting the fever but couldn't desert them.

In the afternoon, two Canadian priests came down into the hold. I felt sorry for them because they were nervous at death in the darkness all around them. The only light was a glow from the lanterns hung on the walls. The stench of soiled clothes and excrement surrounded us. While the one priest ministered to others, Father Moylan, a big strapping priest from Quebec, gave Ma and Da the last rites and closed Da's eyes. He held Ma's hand once Da went. Da died the way he lived, quietly and with dignity.

*　*　*

On the outskirts of the village of Camp, desolate cottages filled the landscape, some tumbled, others empty. Just north of Camp with the waters of Tralee Bay behind it, a mother, trim with hair of strawberry blond, invited them into her cottage for tea. "Have a seat for tea and soda bread, Father, why don't ye? Sure, 'tis a lonesome road you're traveling, and I'd be glad for the company."

Brother Leonard said, "We would like to put our horse and trap in your barn to get it off the road, like."

"Of course, just make sure you close the shed door tightly to make sure the horse is well hidden, or the tinkers may steal it. I'm Nora Johnson and this is Danny, four, and Moira, two. Their Da is away working for The Society of Friends on their farm in Galway. We're blessed that he makes some money and brings us a sack of turnips and some flour from their stores, like. On his trips home, he has to guard the food with his life, even carries a knife if you can believe it, all to keep the hunger from our door."

"Yes, some of the poor are desperate enough. I'm Brother Leonard and this lad is Johnjoe traveling with me to join our order in Tralee."

"'Tis terrible sad to see the poor souls on the road begging, some of them my own neighbors. I give what I can, but it's never enough. People are eating nettles, mountain berries, roots of dandelions and ferns, and the pickings by the seashore. Sure, some of them die on the roads and lie unburied in a ditch, God help us."

The Johnson house was tidy, made of whitewashed stone within and without. Two cane-seated chairs stood next to the hearth with a small bed for the children close to it and a larger bed in the corner over which hung a wooden cross with a bleeding Christ.

"Thank God we're all healthy with the fever about," Mrs. Johnson said. "Some villages are infested with it. The hardest hit are the little ones and the old folk. Sure they bury the dead from an entire village in a single coffin."

IDIOT AND MOTHER.

"The wretched mendicant, with her idiot boy, is an object of deep commiseration. The poorest wretch to whom his mother appeals in his behalf would be almost afraid, in the sight of Heaven, to refuse to divide a handful of meal or potatoes with him. From morning till night his eternal 'pal, la! pal la!' is heard, unless when he stops the cravings of hunger with the offal that is thrown to him by the hand of poverty-stricken charity."

Illustrated London News, August 12, 1843.

From Steve Taylor's website Views of the Famine

http://adminstaff.vassar.edu/sttaylor/FAMINE/

Brother Leonard said, "The fever has now attacked those in the workhouses, overcrowded because of the tumblings."

"Yes," Johnjoe said. "I saw people dying of it in the Dingle workhouse and aboard ship when we were crowded together."

Mrs. Johnson said, "Sure it's gotten so bad I'm afraid to have a poor traveler stay overnight with us for fear he may infect us. The fever has made us neglect ordinary Christian charity."

From the fire Mrs. Johnson drew a black frying pan bearing a steaming loaf of soda bread, brown and crusty on top, moist and filled with raisins on the inside. As she cut slices for them all, she said, "I've a bit of butter if you'd like. In better times we'd have marmalade."

"No, Mrs. Johnson, save the butter for your children. Your bread needs nothing. It's delicious, as good as my mother made," said Brother Leonard.

The woman turned crimson with the praise.

As she cut some for Johnjoe, her little boy and girl, attracted by the smell of the bread, overcame their shyness and came to the table. The two children had their mother's blond hair and blue eyes.

Johnjoe spoke up, "Mrs. Johnson, your bread is wonderful. I love it."

"Well, then, so, I'll carve half a loaf for your journey," the woman replied.

"You will not," chimed in Brother Leonard, "though we're thankful."

"I was just about to bake another loaf anyway," the mother answered. "I insist. Look how the little ones take to Johnjoe, playing with him so easily. Children have a keen sense of goodness in others," said the mother.

At these kind words, Johnjoe felt soft tears make their way down his face. The love and kindness of Mrs. Johnson awoke in Johnjoe memories of his own mother. He yearned again for his Ma and Da as in his mind's eye he relived their last day on the *Ajax*.

When the two travelers rose to leave after their meal, the little boy and girl began to cry at Johnjoe's going. He gave the two children his last shilling. When the mother began to object to his generosity, Johnjoe said, "Missus, please. Allow me to do a small kindness. In just these few minutes you've given me back some of my mother."

Moved by the youth's words, Mrs. Johnson grew misty-eyed. Brother Leonard thought Johnjoe was growing more confident before his eyes. Maybe the young man could survive on his own. Mrs. Johnson wrapped the remainder of the soda bread in a soft cloth and thrust it into Johnjoe's hands, kissing him on the cheek as she did so: "For your trip."

Johnjoe was so surprised he didn't even blush.

Touched by the mother's kindness, Brother Leonard and Johnjoe were quiet on the road. After some minutes Brother Leonard spoke: "What a lesson we've just received. Here is this wonderful mother living in the midst of hunger and death giving us of her substance. Many of the big farmers, the landed gentry, pay no attention to their own starving tenants. Land grabbers, they drive the poor off their land."

"Yes, Brother, she's like my own mother who though dying on board ship thought only of protecting me by keeping me away from her because of the fever."

*   *   *

Lieutenant Benjamin Thomas was the nearest thing to a friend Captain Packenham had in his troop. He accompanied his superior everywhere. Like his captain, he had served in the terrible battle against the Indian rebels at Modkree. Unlike the captain, however, Lieutenant Thomas had survived the fighting unscarred in both body and spirit. Red-haired and angular, the lieutenant obeyed his superior without question, and sympathized with the man who had lost not only his eye, but part of his soul. From now on, he would stay close to his superior and watch for any signs of violence. The captain burned with bitterness. Had Thomas reacted more swiftly, he might have saved the poor wretch the captain killed at the workhouse. The captain was taking the escape of the boy and the Christian Brother personally.

As they rode from Castlegregory to Tralee, the captain showed Thomas the letter he had received from their commander in Dublin:

Captain Packenham:
Find and hang the murderer of Major Mahon immediately. Spare no effort in scouring the country round for the killer. As you know, the major was a member of the Ninth Light Dragoons and a personal friend. London is up in arms over this outrage.
General Penny

"Captain, I know the other landowners in the west of Ireland are fearful. Some have even left the country, and no one is willing to buy the major's 10,000 acres. The white boys have killed five other landlords in the area and wounded one more. But like you, I saw no harm in the boy and the brother when we met them on the road."

"That may be, Lieutenant, but if we don't find them in Tralee, it means that they are trying to run from us."

The day was dark with gray enveloping clouds as the troop made their way into the narrow cobbled streets of Tralee. The bay was to their left wrapping itself around the base of the city. The Christian Brothers taught in a three-story building of gray stone, Artane, an industrial school built like a fortress. A stone crucifix stood atop the roof directly over the entrance. When a brother answered the door, Captain Packenham announced, "We're searching for a man from your order, Brother Leonard, and a young man with him. Brother Leonard told us he was coming here."

"I'm Brother Luke," a man with a farmer's build, replied. "I

51

know Brother Leonard well, but he hasn't come here. I haven't seen him in months."

"I don't believe, you," said the captain, and slammed the brother against the wall. "Stand aside while we search the building."

The six dragoons dispersed throughout the building and the barn in back. They found families occupying what had once been classrooms, the people defeated, waiting for a meal, but no sign of Brother Leonard or the youth.

When the troops had reassembled at the front of the building, the captain told Brother Luke, "You're hiding them."

The brother answered, "We're hiding no one."

Captain Packenham lunged at the brother and grabbed him by the throat, screaming, "I know they're here." The captain was in a universe of his own, his anger overflowing like molten lava.

Lieutenant Thomas feared his superior would make another martyr, so he tried to pry Packenham's hands finger by finger from the choking man. It was no use.

Finally, Lieutenant Thomas leaned in and screamed into the captain's ear, "Patrick, Patrick, leave off. You'll kill the man." Wild-eyed, the captain looked at the lieutenant as an intruder from another world and returned to reality, his victim sputtering at his feet.

"You're liars, all of you clergy," the captain shouted at Brother Luke and stomped from the building.

As the troops left town, the captain recovered his temper, but he found himself in a dilemma. He had to outguess his adversaries, not knowing where they would travel next. Allowing his lieutenant to catch up with him at the head of the troop, the captain muttered, "We've been tricked. Canon Long and Brother Gerald and our two criminals all said they were headed for Tralee, but they didn't come here."

"Captain, something's been nagging me about the boy ever since we stopped them on the road. I didn't have much of a look at him, but I'd seen him before, something about his carriage and demeanor. I think of him in connection with a bloody deed at one of the tumblings."

"Lies, all lies, from these religious. That devious Canon Long is hiding something. I know it. I'll force him to confess."

"Yes, Captain, but no torture. You know how these Irish are about their priests. They're still singing songs about Father Murphy who in 1798 had led the rebels at Boolavogue and was burned at the stake."

"Well, it's important, so comb your memory. When we go back, look over the reports. Something in them may bring the boy to mind."

*   *   *

As the troops retraced their path west towards Dingle, on the road they met a crowd of beggars who gave them wide berth. On impulse the captain stopped and addressed the bedraggled group. He was looking for an informer, that most hated of Irishmen.

"A sovereign to any of you who saw a clergyman and a boy traveling in a horse and buggy."

"I'm your man, Sir," shouted out a middle-aged man in rough clothes forcing his way through the group. "A priest and a boy with him, near Camp."

The man's wife said, "My own husband a dirty informer. May the hearthstone of hell be your bed rest forever," and she marched away from him.

The captain flipped a sovereign to the man who caught it cleanly.

"Another sovereign if you can tell me where they stopped."

"At Mrs. Johnson's just north of town, a clean white-washed cottage."

"Take me there for another coin," exclaimed the captain.

Just around the bend in the road, the man pointed out the house: "Just there, the one in good repair."

The captain flipped his guide the second coin, and the troops rode up to the cottage.

When Nora Johnson opened the door to the captain's knock, she was frightened to see the soldiers. "Yes, Sir."

Packenham said, "We're hunting a cleric and a young man for the murder of Major Mahon."

The mother blessed herself at the mention of the death.

"The neighbors told us they stopped here."

"Yes, Captain, for some tea and soda bread. Yesterday it was."

"Stand aside while we search your home," the captain ordered.

The only other inhabitants of the house were a little boy and girl infected by their mother's fear and clinging to her skirt.

When his men had checked the outbuildings, the captain barked again at the mother: "I wonder where they were headed."

"Tralee, Captain, to the seminary," the mother said.

"Missus, I want the truth. If you're lying to me, you're aiding those criminals, and it will go hard for you and your family."

"Captain, they told me they were on a trip to Tralee for the boy to join the order."

"That's ten miles and we've just come down that road. They had provisions for a journey."

"I don't know, Captain, but I gave them half a loaf of soda bread."

"Missus, for your sake I hope you've been truthful with me."

"I have, Sir."

When the troops rode off, the mother was shaken, drawing her little ones close. In these cruel times, even small kindnesses could bring danger.

*　*　*

Back in their Dingle barracks, Lieutenant Thomas found nothing in his first trawl through the records, all neatly written in the captain's hand. The next morning he approached Bailiff Sheedy. "Bailiff, I've been searching the records hunting for the boy who escaped with

Brother Leonard. In my mind, I associate him with something bloody at his family's ejectment."

"Lieutenant, I can only think of that damned cur that jumped at me at the Kevane house. The captain took care of the dog, spiking it on his bayonet and then cutting it in two."

"Yes, Bailiff, that's it. There was a boy."

"Yes, Lieutenant, a fool of a boy who picked up his dead collie right in front of Captain Packenham's feet. Johnjoe Kevane is his name. He was lucky the captain didn't cut him down, too. But they've gone off to Canada."

Disappointed, Lieutenant Thomas said, "I thought it was the same young man on the road. You saw a youth with Brother Leonard the evening before."

"I did, Lieutenant, but it was dark and he was too far off to make out. The only ones who might know are Brother Leonard and perhaps Canon Long."

"Bailiff, no one has ever returned from Canada."

"Not a one, Sir, and thousands have made that trip, 3000 from Major Mahon's estates alone. They would have to pay for their passage back and make their way here to the west of Ireland. Impossible."

"Thanks, Bailiff."

When Lieutenant Thomas told Packenham of his fruitless search, the captain withdrew even further into himself. All his life he had devoted himself fully to his duty. For years he had battled the Indians in the Punjab. Now he was stuck in this Kerry backwater chasing a murderer who was always just beyond reach. In his soul he was also worried about himself. He felt his self-control and discipline slipping away. He carried out half-hangings and pitch cappings and shot the poor devil at the workhouse. He throttled the brother in Tralee where only Lieutenant Thomas had saved him from one more killing. He wasn't even thinking any more, just lashing out at the world. His Bible failed to console him.

Chapter 7

MULLINS'S HUT, AT SCULL.

"A specimen of the in-door horrors of Scull may be seen in the annexed sketch of the hut of a poor man named Mullins, who lay dying in a corner upon a heap of straw, supplied by the Relief Committee, whilst his three wretched children crouched over a few embers of turf, as if to raise the last remaining spark of life. This poor man, it appears, had buried his wife some five days previously, and was, in all probability, on the eve of joining her, when he was found out by the untiring efforts of the Vicar, who, for a few short days, saved him from that which no kindness could ultimately avert. The Vicar himself died not long after. Our Artist assures us that the dimensions of the hut do not exceed ten feet square; adding that, to make the sketch, he was compelled to stand up to his ankles in the dirt and filth upon the floor. "

Illustrated London News, February 20, 1847.

From Steve Taylor's Website Views of the Famine

http://adminstaff.vassar.edu/sttaylor/FAMINE/

On their way from Camp to Listowel, the two fugitives traveled around Tralee. They passed broken-down cottages in an abandoned village, its inhabitants driven out by landlord evictions. One hovel showed wisps of smoke, the rest of the buildings covered with ivy and thick nettles. Fuchsia, foxglove, honeysuckle, and other wildflowers bloomed over the desolate landscape with a view of Tralee Bay as backdrop. From one of the huts, a teenage girl ran out and said, "Father, Father, please come. I'm Mary Mullins. Me Da is going. He needs you."

Though Brother Leonard wasn't a priest and couldn't administer the sacraments, out of kindness he and Johnjoe followed the girl. Extreme unction was the last sacrament a Catholic received before death, calling for absolution of the sins of the penitent and a blessing. The brother had no reason to tell the girl that he wasn't a priest. She might not understand because he wore a Roman collar. All she wanted was spiritual and human comfort.

Lying on some straw under a roof half open to the sky, a man in his thirties was breathing in short bursts.

"Johnjoe, see can you scour up some peat and wood for the fire."

"See, Father, it's the death rattle. He's going the same as my Ma. Bless him, please," Mary asked.

Brother Leonard recited a Latin prayer for the dying: *"Misereatur tui omnipotens Deus, et dimissis peccatis tuis, perducat te ad vitam aeternam."* Then he recited the same prayer in English for the girls and Johnjoe to follow: "May almighty God have mercy on you, and having forgiven your sins lead you to eternal life."

Johnjoe and the girls responded, "Amen."

The peat and wood Johnjoe had brought helped stoke the fire, but with the roof partly open, it was as cold and damp inside the cottage as without. Brother Leonard knew that the dying man would not last long as his breathing became shallower. To give the little girls some warmth, Johnjoe took his coat and wrapped it around them.

He sat with them on the stone floor as they hovered near the embers of the fire and watched their father die.

Mary said to Brother Leonard, "Me Ma died with the fever last week, and now Da is going. I don't know how we'll survive, me and the little ones."

Brother Leonard patted the girl's hand and said, "We'll take you to Father Cavanagh's in Listowel."

The girl was relieved to have someone promise help and share the deathwatch with her.

After some time Brother Leonard reached behind Mr. Mullins and brought his chest forward to make his dying breath easier.

Mary said, "He's gone, Father."

"Yes, he's at peace."

Mary cried, but her sisters, Josie and Nellie, were numb and silent.

Brother Leonard gently closed the man's eyes and put the man's arms across his chest, and they all recited the rosary, after which he placed his beads in the man's hands. They sat for a while, the nearest thing Michael Mullins would have to a wake.

"We'll leave your Da like that until we bury him tomorrow," Brother Leonard said. "Mary, fetch a blanket or sheet to cover him. We'll put rocks on the corners to make the shroud tight for fear of rats and dogs. All of us can fit in the buggy for the ride to Listowel."

*   *   *

Listowel, once a thriving market town, sat on the banks of the River Feale, a dense woods just east of it, one of the few stands of trees left pristine by the English as they raped Ireland's forests for timber to ship home. Much more suitable for farming, the land here was hilly but not mountainous as in Dingle.

Father Cavanagh, a lean man in his fifties with a shock of gray hair, answered Brother Leonard's knock, surprised to see the brother with his charges. "Leonard and the three Mullins girls whose mother I buried last week."

"We attended their Da as he died. The girls are on their own and need our help."

"Come in, come in. Let me feed you," said the priest. "You look starved with the hunger."

"Father, I'm Johnjoe Kevane. I would like to put the horse and buggy in your barn to be off the road."

"Of course, next to my own. Hay is piled in the barn, and you can draw water from the well for your horse. Mind you lock the door from those thieving tinkers. They're always looking out for horses, sheep, and cows."

The priest's rectory was a small square farmhouse of yellow stucco. Across the road was his school, St. Michael's, two floors of gray stone, now converted into a soup kitchen and dormitory for children of evicted tenants, most of them now orphans.

"I'll fetch some stirabout from the school for your supper, and we'll eat in my small kitchen," said Father Cavanagh. "Now stand by the fire, all of you, till I come back."

The priest returned in the company of a nun, Sister Clare, a member of the Sisters of Mercy. Father Cavanagh had recruited her from Dublin through an old friend Sister Catherine McAuley, founder of the order. Tall and strong, Sister Clare was a farmer's daughter, built for work. She and the priest carried over two small pots of stirabout, ground Indian corn maize and American rice brought by the Quakers. She was all work, feeding the children and hunting down fresh clothes for them. The Mullins girls gulped down their soup and some bread Sister Clare had baked.

"Now Mary, Josie, and Nellie," the nun said, "you've had a terrible time of it losing both your parents, but they would want you to live. I'm going to give you all a good cleaning with hot water in a room off the dormitory. We'll scrub with soap and cut your beautiful hair to catch any head lice because you've come from a house with the fever. We have bonnets and shawls to cover your heads for the Mass and burial. It's important to stay clean and healthy. Tomorrow morning we'll bury your Da next to your Ma, and Johnjoe and I will be with you every step of the way. Think of him as your older brother."

The girls would sob when their ebony hair was shaved from their heads, but they had found people who were kind to them.

When Sister Clare and the girls left for the school after their meal, Father Cavanagh, Brother Leonard, and Johnjoe sat around the kitchen talking. "But for Sister Clare and the kindness of the Quakers, I don't know what I'd do. Many more of us would be dead. Leonard, I haven't had two minutes to talk to you and Johnjoe. I have a jug of poteen, good strong drink, brewed for me by a farmer friend. I'm dying for a glass. Please share a drink with me."

"I will indeed, Father. I haven't had a drink in months."

"Johnjoe, I'll pour you a touch just for the taste of it."

The boy was grateful to be included. His father had given him a wee bit of poteen at Christmas one year. Made of fermented yeast, the drink was strong, doubly precious to the Irish because it was powerful and illegal, made to avoid the British distillery tax.

When Johnjoe went across the road to the boys' dormitory to sleep, Brother Leonard sat with the priest by the fire and unfolded Johnjoe's story. "He's a good lad, Father, and the shooting was at least doubtful, the major charging at him with his whip. But we've run from the dragoons, throwing suspicion on both of us, like."

"Good God, Leonard, you're putting yourself and the brothers in such danger for a murderer. You may have taken too much on yourself."

"Father, I've taught him and know his goodness despite what he's done. If we're trouble to you, we'll leave, and I'll find some place else for us. I've prayed over this and know I'm doing right."

"Leonard, you're a kind man. You should join those brothers in

Newfoundland. You can do good work there with our exiles. Write your superior general for permission. It would distance you from the trouble in Dingle. As for Johnjoe, he must be resourceful. No one has ever survived a coffin ship and returned home."

"He wants to be off on his own. He'll be a fine man if the dragoons don't put a noose on him. In just a few days, he seems to have grown from boy to man. He was a help to me with the Mullins girls, caring for them and giving them strength. Somehow we'll have to get Canon Long's horse and trap back to him."

"I'll take care of that, Leonard."

Johnjoe was up before dawn and fed their own horse and Father Cavanagh's. Then he drew water from the well for both horses. When the priest walked into the barn, he said, "You're not afraid of work, lad."

"I'm a farm boy, Father."

"I see."

"Father, I have something to ask you. I feel responsible for the Mullins girls. I want to stay close to them for a while to keep an eye on them, like. I could do tasks here in the barn and mend some fences. I would like to stay in the dormitory while I work for you. I want no pay other than a roof over my head and some stirabout to keep me fit."

"That's a grand idea. I spend so much time burying the dead that I have no time to maintain this place, which is falling down over my head. You would be a Godsend to me."

"Thanks, Father. Now I'm sure Brother Leonard told you about me. If I were ever a danger to you and your work, I'd be off right away."

"Don't trouble yourself about that. Yes, I know your story, but I judge a man as I find him, not by his history. I find nothing but goodness in you."

Over breakfast, Father Cavanagh, Brother Leonard and Johnjoe made plans for the funeral of Michael Mullins. "Leonard and Johnjoe, take my horse and buggy because it's bigger than yours and go to the coroner in town for a drop-lid coffin. A hideous thing it is, with a hinge on the bottom opened by a lever, allowing the body to drop straight in the grave. One poor boy, Tom Guerin, was buried alive. In some sort of coma he was until the thump of the shovel roused him, and he was dug out with two broken legs."

"Yes, Father, I heard the tale," said Brother Leonard. "Johnjoe and I will put the father into the coffin. Please God no rats or dogs have got at it. We'll close the coffin up for fear those poor girls will want to touch their Da, placing themselves at risk for infection. I don't know what will become of the girls."

"14,000 orphan girls between fourteen and eighteen are sailing to Australia to find work and husbands there, but I haven't the heart to send these girls away, especially just after losing their parents," the priest said.

Johnjoe said, "On board ship I heard of a group in New York that takes Irish girls in and provides them with good employment: The Mission of Our Lady of the Rosary for the Protection of Irish Immigrant Girls."

"A good idea, but these Mullins girls are too young," said Father Cavanagh. "The Sisters of Mercy have an orphanage for girls in Dublin. They may have room for them next year. I'll ask Sister Clare. For now they can live here."

"Johnjoe and I will fetch the body from the cottage and bring it to the church," said Brother Leonard.

"As for the two of ye, bring a bucket of water and soap to clean yourselves after touching the body, mind," said Father Cavanagh.

At noon after Johnjoe and Brother Leonard had brought the coffin to the church, Father Cavanagh said the Mass for the Dead. Those children living in the school dormitories attended along with some of the local farmers, all praying that they not share the fate of Michael Mullins and become infected with typhus.

At the Mass Johnjoe served as altar boy, bringing the cruets of water and wine to the priest and responding to the Latin prayers he had learned as a child. The priest gave no sermon because Father Cavanagh had run out of things to say about the deaths in his flock. As Johnjoe held the Communion plate under each face, shriveled with hunger, the priest thought of the meaning of the liturgical words, "I am the bread of life"— this to a starving people.

After Mass everyone walked to the Listowel cemetery close by, Brother Leonard and Johnjoe acting as pallbearers. Father Cavanagh said a final prayer, and the coroner pulled a lever opening the hinged-bottom, releasing the body into the grave. Buried from the same coffin as his wife, Michael Mullins lay next to her. Johnjoe and Brother Leonard filled in the gravesite.

The Mullins girls stood huddled with Sister Clare, but as they walked back to St. Michael's, the two youngest girls detached themselves from her and held Johnjoe's hand. In two days he had become their older brother.

While the group trudged along, Father Cavanagh and Sister Clare in front, Johnjoe and the girls just behind, a heavy-set man on a huge brown horse rode up beside Father Cavanagh. "Another burial, I see," said William Gray, a prominent Protestant landowner, a jumper to the Church of England. "Well, it's your own fault. This is God's providence at work, paying ye back for Catholic popery, punishing ye for your sins of Romish religious superstition, like the plague God sent on the Egyptians."

"Mr. Gray, it's privileged you are indeed to have such special insight into God's plans," Father Cavanagh said.

"Don't use your sarcasm with me. You Catholics even take money from the godless Indian, $170 from the Choctaw tribe in Oklahoma. Just look around you. This is God's wrath for allowing the Church of Rome to flourish here. Indeed, this is a blessed Famine. The Catholics must die off. God be praised."

"Yes, so you will have more room to graze sheep for your wool trade," said Father Cavanagh.

"God helps those who help themselves," said Mr. Gray.

63

Johnjoe had heard enough. He excused himself from the Mullins sisters, got a running start, and with the flat of his hand gave the horse a mighty smack on the rump, sending it galloping down the road, Mr. Gray barely able to hang on.

"Well done," said Father Cavanagh, as he couldn't help but laugh at the trouble Gray's mouth brought him again. "What that big walloper Gray was on about is that The Choctaw Indians from Oklahoma, God bless them, sent $170 to help us. The American government moved them 600 miles from Georgia to Oklahoma, the "Trail of Tears" it's called. They lost half their people. They understand suffering, unlike Mr. Gray."

* * *

For the next few weeks Johnjoe set himself to work shoring up the timbers in the barn and mending broken fences for the sheep grazing. Despite his initial reservations about the young man, Father Cavanagh found him to be just as he appeared—honest and hard working. In what free time he had, Johnjoe continued writing in his diary, bringing it out with him during his long days with the sheep. He took care of the flock, much easier here than in mountainous Ballyristeen. When a farmer gave Father Cavanagh a pup from a litter of border collies, Johnjoe trained it to rein in the sheep by nipping at their legs. The dog was a tonic for him, but in his heart he had never forgiven Captain Packenham for butchering his own dog back home. Johnjoe settled into a routine, free for a time from the need to run from the dragoons. He slept in the boys' dormitory at St. Michael's where he could check in on the girls, always teasing Sister Clare, "You're not feeding them enough. Not an ounce of flesh on them." The nun played along with his gibes, often chasing him from her kitchen with a ladle. The girls loved it. Someone cared.

Chapter 8

After a week at St. Michael's on a Sunday afternoon before their dinner of stirabout, Johnjoe fought with Tommy Linnane, son of an evicted farmer who had died of the fever, leaving the boy and two sisters, Maureen and Eileen. Tommy said to Johnjoe, "Sure, you're always mooning over those Mullins girls. A little too skinny for my taste. But I suppose you've taken a fancy to them. What's the old saying, 'the younger the chicken, the easier, the pickin?'"

Johnjoe cracked the boy in the mouth, sending him sprawling across the polished wooden floor of the dormitory just as Father Cavanagh arrived on the scene.

The priest said, "It's enough we're fighting the English without pounding on each other. Save your energy, or I'll punish you."

"Yes, Father," both boys said.

The next day when Johnjoe returned to the dormitory early from work, he found Tommy pawing through his diary.

"You mention Major Mahon," Tommy said as Johnjoe snatched his diary back.

"It's no business of yours," said Johnjoe. "If you touch this book again, you'll be wearing two black eyes, punishment or no."

But Tommy's interest was piqued. He hated Johnjoe and would get at the book again.

That afternoon Johnjoe found Sister Clare in the kitchen alone. She threw all her energies into cooking and teaching the girls sewing.

"I suppose you are going to pester me about more food for the girls, Johnjoe," Sister Clare said.

"No, Sister. A favor. I've been keeping a diary about my family and me since the dragoons destroyed our house. It's private, but I'm hoping the Quakers will publish it when it's completed. I would like you to read it and give me your opinion. Some of the things in it might shock you. If so, just hide it for me. I caught Tommy with it in the dormitory yesterday, and I want to keep it for the Quakers."

"Of course, I'll hide it away in my room. When you want to write more, come and ask me for it," said Sister Clare.

* * *

In *The Freeman's Journal,* the national paper of Ireland, George Browne, the Bishop of Elphin, attacked the eviction policies of Major Mahon, and printed the names of 3006 people who had sailed on coffin ships and were now dead. On the list were the names "Johnjoe Kevane" and his parents. The bishop listed all the names of those evicted, unaware that he had included a ghost. One July evening as Johnjoe returned from his shepherding, Father Cavanagh met him by the rectory. "I'm talking to a ghost. Look here." The bishop listed all the names of those evicted, unaware that he had included a ghost.

When *The Freeman's Journal* arrived in Dingle, Canon Long was saddened to see the deaths of so many of his former parishioners evicted by Major Mahon. The one bit of good news was that Johnjoe was listed as dead. That might put Captain Packenham off the scent for a time, but the priest was not assured. The danger of an informer lurked everywhere.

* * *

Up to now Tommy Linnane had shown little interest in the Mullins girls. But he became friendlier. "Mary," he said, "I heard Johnjoe's parents died of fever."

"Yes, but he called it ship fever. They died on board ship in Canada," Mary said.

"I wonder how he made his way here," Tommy said.

"Ask him, but I know his name was on the list of Bishop Browne's evictions in the paper Sister Clare showed us," Mary said.

Tommy went immediately to Sister Clare to confirm this news. "Mary said Johnjoe's name was in the paper."

"Look here to me, Tommy. I know you don't like Johnjoe, and he doesn't like you. But if you cause him one spot of trouble by nosing around, I'll break every bone in your carcass." To emphasize her words, she lifted him straight up off the ground and shoved him against the wall until he turned pink.

"Sure, it's just talk, Sister," Tommy choked out.

"You're a liar, Tommy. Mind you keep an eye out for me."

* * *

In what free time she had, Sister Clare took up Johnjoe's diary, not knowing exactly what to expect. She thought the writing might be simple and smack of school exercises, but she was surprised to find a narrative and a personal style. Johnjoe had her start where he had broken off reading to Brother Leonard.

Chapter 9

Village of Moveen

"Sixteen thousand and odd persons unhoused in the Union of Kilrush before the month of June in the present year; seventy one thousand one hundred and thirty holdings done away with in Ireland, and nearly as many homes destroyed in 1848; two hundred and fifty-four thousand holdings of more than one acre and less than five acres put an end to between 1841 and 1848; six-tenths in fact, of the lowest class of tenant driven from their now roofless or annihilated cabins and houses, makes up the general description of that desolation of which Tullig and Moveen are examples. The ruin is great and complete."

Illustrated London News, December 15, 1849 - February 9, 1850

From Steve Taylor's website Views of the Famine

http://adminstaff.vassar.edu/sttaylor/FAMINE/

November 1

Father Moylan got me passage home from Gross Ile by getting me a job on a timber ship headed for Tralee. When the *Jeanie Johnston* reached Tralee, the ship's bursar paid me fifteen pounds for my work. After more than a year away, I was almost home. I started the thirty-mile trek toward Dingle, the ocean and Dingle Bay to the south as I headed west into the setting sun. The countryside was green and beautiful; the sun was shining, but darkness filled my heart.

Guilt gnawed at me for what I was about to do. I hoped that Mahon was already dead, saving me the job of killing him. As I walked along the road to Anascaul, the town before Dingle, I saw that more houses had been torn down, stones and partial walls blackened by fire. Poor starving youth were trying to scour the fields for any morsel of potato or turnip.

BOY AND GIRL AT CAHERA.

"The first Sketch is taken on the road, at Cahera, of a famished boy and girl turning up the ground to seek for a potato to appease their hunger. 'Not far from the spot where I made this sketch,' says Mr. Mahoney, 'and less than fifty perches from the high road, is another of the many sepulchres above ground, where six dead bodies had lain for twelve days, without the least chance of interment, owing to their being so far from the town.'"

Illustrated London News, February 20, 1847.

From Steve Taylor's Website Views of the Famine

http://adminstaff.vassar.edu/sttaylor/FAMINE/

I met a farmer, Paddy Driscoll, on the road carrying a load of hay on his horse and wagon. Offering me a ride, Driscoll struck up a conversation: "Not from these parts are you, lad."

"I'm from Dingle after being away more than a year. I've been working aboard a timber ship."

"You mean to tell me that you've been away from here and are now coming back when the rest of the country is leaving." Driscoll said.

"Yes, Dingle is home."

*　*　*

Sister Clare was so moved by the diary that she put it aside for a while. She felt she had accompanied Johnjoe on the voyage to Grosse Ile. She shared his pain, but the story drained her. She wondered how the young man hadn't lost his mind after all he had endured. She didn't think she would have been as strong. Her remedy for feeling low was to immerse herself in work. She bustled about in the kitchen to bake bread and make stirabout and then went upstairs to supervise the girls with their knitting.

Three weeks after he had begun his stay at St. Michael's, Brother Leonard received a letter from his superior general in Dublin with orders to sail from Cobh with three other brothers to St. John's in Newfoundland to establish a school and an orphanage there, Mt.

Cashel. Many Irish emigrants had settled in Newfoundland, those too poor for the passage to America or Canada.

Brother Leonard said to Johnjoe, "I'm sure we can find a way to get you on board with us."

"No, Brother, but thanks. The Lord Himself could not have been kinder to me than you. Maybe you can get back to teaching there instead of feeding. But here I have the chance to write my story, and even have an idea about how to get it printed."

The Irish aren't huggers, too shy for that, but Johnjoe pulled Brother Leonard to him, tears gracing both faces.

When Brother Leonard left for Cobh, Johnjoe realized he was once more alone in the world. The thought both depressed and relieved him. Brother Leonard had shepherded him through the dragoons. But he would no longer fear for the brother's capture by the dragoons as an accomplice in his flight, Johnjoe now free to carve out his own future.

* * *

After learning of Brother Leonard and Johnjoe's visit to Mrs. Johnson in Camp, Captain Packenham and Lieutenant Thomas headed straight for Canon Long's rectory, the lieutenant watchful for any violence from his superior.

Sitting in the small parlor of the rectory with a peat fire glowing, the captain said, "Well, Canon, we're still looking for the murderer."

Canon Long gave nothing away. "Maybe you've sent him and his family off to Canada."

"That doesn't mean he couldn't have come back."

"Captain, of all the thousands you've driven away, no one could make it back here. That's 3,000 miles each way and months aboard ship. According to *The Freeman's Journal*, if only ye were as good at getting back as you are at sending off: '9992 calves and 822,681 gallons of butter while 400,000 Irish die of starvation, all in the name of 'free market, laissez-faire economies.'"

"Our government's fiscal policy is no concern of mine, Canon. I'm paid by the Crown to uphold the law," said Captain Packenham.

"And a fine law it is that steals food from a starving people to send to England. And just to make sure we go hungry, you send 15,000 additional soldiers here to live off our substance."

"I want the young man, Canon."

"I haven't got him."

"I can make a martyr of you like Father Murphy burned to a stake in '98."

"I'm in no hurry to be a martyr, but I'm not afraid of dying. I don't know where the youth is."

The captain rushed the priest and flung him against the parlor wall, jarring a wooden crucifix to the floor. Suddenly the captain stopped as Lieutenant Thomas rushed up. "You're lucky, Canon, that Lieutenant Thomas is here to restrain me. You're safe—for now." The two dragoons departed from the rectory leaving a dazed Canon Long.

Back on the road, Lieutenant Thomas said to the captain, "What the canon said was true. For every shipment of grain into Ireland, six leave with the same cargo, our own dragoons guarding the ships. More corn is exported from Ireland in one month than was imported in an entire year from America."

"I know, Lieutenant, but that's not our concern."

"But, Patrick, the Irish 'potato people' are starving. I've heard the poor resort to what they called 'bleeding,' draining some of a cow's blood and mixing it with the rotten potatoes and cabbage to make soup."

"Lieutenant, I see the same things as you, but I'm not going to debate England's domestic policies with you. I'm married to my duty. I want the young man."

* * *

On Sunday after Mass, Johnjoe asked Father Cavanagh if he might take the Mullins girls fishing. "Mind, you don't let the warden catch you. That's a fine of thirty shillings, which we don't have. A road on the far side of the river just past the five-arch bridge leads to a good spot. Take my rod; the river bends just beyond the bridge encircled by woods. You can't be seen from above because of the trees and brush."

Johnjoe made fishing poles for each of the three Mullins girls from long pieces of sticks he found about the farm. Even though they were always hungry, from the regular meals of stirabout and bread the girls were able to fill out. As they walked down the road to the River Feale, a canopy of plane trees on either side hung over their heads.

Mary said to Johnjoe, "I hope me Ma and Da are in heaven now."

"I'm sure of it, the same as my Ma and Da, killed with the fever, too."

"Your parents died on ship."

"Yes, far away in Canada, but like you and your sisters I was with them and comforted them when they died."

Johnjoe and the girls arrived at the bank of the river, which rushed over brown boulders and stones, leaving eddying pools in its wake.

When Johnjoe felt a tug on his line, he passed his rod to Nellie, the youngest of the girls. "Take this, and hold on, while I dig up some more worms."

"A fish," Nellie yelled, nearly dropping the rod. Johnjoe scurried over to help her.

"It's probably a twig," Mary said.

"No, indeed, a fat brown trout for our dinner," Johnjoe said.

On his own Johnjoe snared three more trout when the voice of

Father Cavanagh roared down from the road above them, overly loud for Johnjoe and the girls to hear.

"Warden Walsh, out chasing down poachers, I expect."

"Yes, Father, the Queen's fish, you know. I'm about to check the bank down below."

"That's a pity, Warden. Back at the rectory I have a fine jug of poteen, good country drink, that I was going to invite you to sample."

"I would, Father, but I have to search here. I can't see the water because of the trees and brambles. Farmer Driscoll told me he saw some youngsters with fishing rods."

"Well, duty first, Warden, but the poteen may not last the night. Well, no matter, in a few months I may get it again."

"You know, Father, that Driscoll is a windbag. I'm sure no one's fishing down there."

"Warden, I'd be delighted for your company. Let's hurry on to the rectory for a little touch, just the two of us."

Johnjoe and the girls waited for a few minutes and then hurried back to St. Michael's with their trout.

Johnjoe settled into a schedule: up before dawn, milking the one cow, feeding the horses, and then eating his breakfast, usually stirabout and some bread when they had it. He would visit his "ladies" as he called the Mullins girls. He filled the rest of his day grazing the sheep, tending Father Cavanagh's garden of peas and carrots, and writing in his diary. For the first time in months, he was content and falling in love with Mary Mullins.

Chapter 10

The GREAT HUNGER 1845-48

Potato Famine in Ireland

1.500,000 died of starvation & 1,000,000 emigrated. Irish Friends were entrusted with international relief funds to feed the starving, replenish seed & to redeem fishing nets & tools which had been pawned for food.

Quaker Tapestry Scheme©

Visits were made to the areas in most need, mainly in the west, where the potato had become virtually the only food of most of the population. Food was distributed to the needy, whatever their religion, with no strings attached. Soup kitchens were set up in towns and huge quantities were provided – you will see a small plaque in the wall of Monkstown Meeting House where it was dispensed. In today's money the assistance given was about euro14m, much of which came from Friends in other countries, and Friends also expended a huge amount of their own time and energy. At that time there were about 3,000 Friends in Ireland out of a population of 8.5m. During and after the Famine large quantities of seeds for other food crops were distributed and grants were made to fishermen to repair and replace boats and nets. Agricultural training was also provided, and a model farm was established in Co. Galway.

Having decided that he should do what he could to give people the means of avoiding Famine in the future, James Ellis, a Quaker businessman from Bradford, retired early in 1849 and moved to Letterfrack in Co. Galway, where he and his wife Mary used their resources to provide employment and training to scores of men and give schooling to their children. Some of the buildings still exist, and when you visit Letterfrack you will still find much evidence of what they did there.

The Religious Society of Friends (Quakers) in Ireland

"The Quaker Tapestry is a modern embroidery of 77 fascinating panels. Made by 4,000 men, women, and children, this international community project explores three centuries of social history. The Exhibition Centre in Kendal, Cumbria UK is open to the public from early spring to late autumn each year. For more information, visit the website www.quaker-tapestry.co.uk."

One May afternoon a Quaker of late middle age, with two of his fellows on horseback, rode up to St. Michael's to deliver a wagonload of corn meal and rice. They were all dressed in the Quaker tradition of brown and gray with no buttons, ribbons, or other adornment. Father Cavanagh had told Johnjoe that during the Famine the Quakers imported almost one thousand tons of foodstuffs from America, saving the lives of hundreds of thousands of Irish. "Hello there, young man," the Quaker said to Johnjoe. "I'm Joseph Bewley. I've brought a load of corn and rice for Father Cavanagh."

"Yes, Mr. Bewley, Father told me to look out for you. He's out on a sick call attending a man dying with the fever. If your two companions will help me, I'd be happy to unload the corn and rice while you wait in the rectory for Father."

"Thanks, lad. I'll do that and get a bit of a rest. Yesterday we served 1,500 gallons of soup in Skibbereen, and I'm tired."

"God bless you, Sir," said Johnjoe. "Sister Clare will be thrilled to have the food."

Father Cavanagh had told Johnjoe that he had nothing but praise for Joseph Bewley, a successful Dublin merchant who owned and operated a number of coffee and teashops. During the Famine, Father Cavanagh explained, Bewley threw himself fully into the work of feeding the starving Irish. In 1846 during the worst of the Famine, he founded the Central Relief Committee that worked from Dublin. The CRC had purchased at cost 294 steam boilers from a Quaker company in Liverpool, Abraham and Alfred Darby. When the Dublin Quakers wished to pay the full price, the Darbys refused. The CRC had distributed them throughout Ireland for cooking soup in the workhouses and other centers.

From Father Cavanagh, Johnjoe also learned that the CRC funneled most American donations to Ireland. The Irish Quakers paid no attention to one's religion, unlike some Irish Baptists who demanded religious conversion or church attendance for food, the Irish branding the practice "souperism." The Quakers were also sensitive to the people's need for dignity, which they respected by charging a pence a quart for their soup, rather than just giving it away.

By the time Johnjoe and the two men unloaded the corn and rice, Father Cavanagh had returned, and invited the men and Johnjoe in for tea. When they went into the parlor, Bewley was fast asleep. The priest decided to let the man rest and have their tea in Sister Clare's kitchen, the nun herself upstairs teaching.

When Bewley woke after almost an hour, he found Father Cavanagh and the other Quakers across the road in St. Michael's.

"Another dying, I suppose, Father," said Mr. Bewley, still groggy from his nap in front of the fire.

"Yes, Joseph, but not quite yet. I gave him the last rites, but he won't last long, I'm afraid. But for ye Quakers more of us would be gone."

"Thanks, Father, but it's so little we can do. My friend, James Tuke, told me he found a cabin in Carrick-on-Suir with the door shut. He had the curiosity to open it where he found a family of four lying together. The father was decomposed; the mother the last to die had closed the door. The custom when all hope is gone is to get into the darkest corner and die out of the eyes of passersby."

Father Cavanagh, Johnjoe, and the other two Quakers listened to the tale with sadness, knowing it was true.

"Joseph, doesn't it make you wonder if God exists at all," said Father Cavanagh as he drank his tea.

"Yes, Father."

Noting Bewley's tiredness, the priest was worried about him. "I wonder how you stand the travel and all the work."

"I manage, Father. The real heroes are the women. They work in the soup kitchens, distribute clothing, and teach in the industrial schools—sewing, making lace and fishnets, and other crafts, and most importantly they hold our families together. A wonderful American woman, a widow, Mrs. Nicholson, uses her own money for Famine relief and some funds we give her."

"You've saved thousands of lives."

"Father, thanks, but we have a terrible time with the government in London. Prime Minister Russell asked us to take over the 130 workhouses in the west of the country, and we have to turn him down because he won't give us the food or money we need. Our religion teaches us personal responsibility and stewardship for our bleeding nation, virtues the English lack."

Johnjoe and the others listened intently.

Bewley went on. "The government in London believes in a laissez-faire economy, that the Irish should take care of themselves, but the poor have nothing standing between them and death. Our resources are dwindling, our collections bringing in less and less. In London they speak of 'Famine fatigue' and 'compassion fatigue'. I wish they were here on the ground to see what things are really like."

"Mr. Bewley," said Johnjoe, "you Quakers have done a wonderful job of telling the world of our starvation and disease in newspapers, publishing the news in periodicals, pamphlets, and even speaking before Parliament. I've written an account of my family and our time aboard a Famine ship. It's nearly complete. I'm wondering if you would help me get it printed."

"But, lad, you're too young to be a writer. I don't know if you would have the skill and experience."

"Sir," Johnjoe said, "I'm just after returning from Grosse Ile."

Bewley was shocked and looked at Father Cavanaugh who nodded his head in confirmation. "You came back from that island of death."

The other Quakers were amazed.

"Yes, Sir."

"That's a miracle, lad. No one has ever come back. Of course, we would help you publish your account, but the writing must be authentic, mind."

"My story is plain and accurate," said Johnjoe.

"We would certainly be interested in looking at it," said Mr. Bewley. "The only first-hand account of those ships is the letter written to Parliament by Mr. Stephen De Vere, an Irish Member of Parliament from Limerick, who volunteered to live two months in steerage aboard an emigrant vessel to Canada—just to see what conditions were. I have it with me." Drawing a copy of *The Freeman's Journal* from a brown satchel, Bewley read the letter. "Hundreds of poor people huddled together without Light, without Air, wallowing in filth and breathing a fetid Atmosphere, sick in Body, dispirited in Heart, the fevered Patients lying between the Sound, to imbibe the contagion; living without food or medicine, except as administered by the hand of casual charity, dying without the voice of spiritual consolation, and buried in the deep without the rites of the church."

Tears leaked from Johnjoe's eyes. "That's what it was like, Mr. Bewley. The man has it right." Father Cavanagh leaned over and patted Johnjoe's arm.

"When you've finished your diary, we'll get it to Dublin to look at. If it's good and true, we'll print it. We've heard of a man in Boston publishing his diary of a coffin ship, too, Robert Whyte."

"Yes, Sir. He was on my voyage and gave me a leather book to write in," said Johnjoe. "He allowed me to copy some of his writing and advised me how to tell our story."

"That's all to the good, Johnjoe. Your stories can verify each other," said Mr. Bewley. "We'd love to look at it for publication."

"And timely, too," said Father Cavanagh. "Bishop Joseph Signay from Quebec wrote a letter reprinted in *The Irish Independent* to all Irish bishops and priests that already more than five thousand human beings have been consigned to their eternal rest in the Catholic cemetery in Grosse Ile. And his letter touched even Parliament who is trying to place physicians on board emigrant ships, and they're adding more officers at points of embarkation, and charging ship owners for medical inspections."

"Those are positive steps," said Mr. Bewley.

As Mr. Bewley and his two Quaker assistants were leaving St. Michael's after their tea, Johnjoe went to gather in the sheep for the night. Two men rode up on horseback to the rectory, Mr. Gray and Sheriff Costello. Gray quickly dismounted and accosted Father Cavanagh.

"I want that tramp of a boy," demanded Gray, bullying his way through the three Quakers.

"I've got a dormitory full of boys," said Father Cavanagh, "just across the road. We're feeding them, with no help from you."

"I don't appreciate your invective."

"Your church must never heed the story of Dives and Lazarus, the Rich Man and the Poor Man, told by the Lord Himself," said Father Cavanagh. "You might look to it."

"That's an insult," said Mr. Gray.

"What's an insult is a nation starving because of your greed," said Father Cavanagh.

"Let the Irish poor take care of themselves," said Gray, echoing the words of Secretary of the Treasury Trevelyan, 'that there is only one way in which the relief of the destitute has been or ever will be, conducted consistently with the general welfare, and that is by making it a local charge.'

"The parable of Dives and Lazarus gets short shrift in England, too," said Father Cavanagh.

"I want the boy who startled my horse," Mr. Gray said.

"You can search the dormitory and fields," Father Cavanagh said.

"Sheriff, fetch the boy," ordered Gray.

Mr. Bewley and his Quaker assistants, ardent pacifists, were nevertheless curious to see how this conflict would end, and waited talking to Father Cavanagh, while Gray paraded on his horse back and forth in front of St. Michael's like an overstuffed Napoleon. Bewley had taken to Johnjoe and wanted no trouble for him.

When the sheriff returned with Johnjoe driving his sheep before him, Gray was frenzied. "That's the scoundrel, could have been the death of me. He swatted my horse and sent it clattering down the road. I could have been killed."

Sheriff Costello said to Johnjoe, "You spooked Mr. Gray's horse."

"Not purposely, Sir."

"Explain what you mean," said the sheriff.

"I saw a blue-arsed horsefly as big as an acorn biting the poor beast. They torture the horses, so to save the animal any more suffering I smashed the fly against the horse's rump."

Even Sheriff Costello had to smirk.

"That's outrageous," blustered Gray. "A lie."

"Any witnesses?" the sheriff asked Gray.

"Just this charlatan of a priest here and some ragamuffin children," Gray said.

"Three little girls coming back from their father's funeral

81

having to listen to your praise for the blessed Famine,'" said Father Cavanagh.

"'A blessed Famine', is it Mr. Gray? My brother and his four little ones died last month of starvation and fever in Roscommon," said the now furious sheriff.

Looking for someone to blame for the turn of events, Gray focused on Johnjoe. "Tinker bastard." He slashed Johnjoe with his horsewhip, raising two ugly welts on his face. Before Gray could strike a third time, Johnjoe grabbed the leather crop in mid-air, yanking Gray from his horse. He landed all a flutter in the middle of the road before an audience of the visiting Quakers and children from St. Michael's.

Johnjoe said, "I should use your own lash on you." But he didn't. Instead he struck the horse on his hindquarters and sent it galloping down the road. He then flung the crop as far as he could into the sheep field.

Father Cavanagh said to Johnjoe, "See Sister Clare about your cuts."

Trying to salvage some dignity, Gray dusted himself off and could only threaten: "You'll pay for this all of you."

Father Cavanagh called after him, "Don't come back here. All you are is trouble."

The priest went over to console Sheriff Costello. "It's sorry I am about your family. If you wouldn't object, I'll say a Mass for them."

"Thanks, Father. In these times, we should ignore differences of religion. Let me know the day and time of the Mass, and my family and I will attend."

"I would like to offer you a touch of poteen for the sake of hospitality," said Father Cavanagh.

"Yes, indeed," said the sheriff. "Gray tries my patience."

Johnjoe drove the sheep across the road to the barn. With his companions, Mr. Bewley set out for Skibbereen, thinking to himself that Johnjoe could help some day in the Quaker relief efforts. He had a forceful presence, maybe even leadership potential.

* * *

"I heard you took those girls fishing," said Tommy Linnane to Johnjoe as they dressed in the dormitory before breakfast.

"Yes."

"The oldest one is right smart, especially when her raven hair grows back. I love her freckles, but she's still too skinny for me. When it's warmer you can take them swimming, see what she really has, like."

"Mother of God, but you're a slow learner," said Johnjoe as he smashed the boy over his right eye.

Tommy bounced up and bloodied Johnjoe's nose. The punch ignited Johnjoe who hit the boy with a flurry of lefts and rights. Soon other boys from the dormitory formed a cheering circle around the two combatants. The more Johnjoe fought, the angrier he became. Finally he stopped. Tommy was defenseless, with two black eyes and other cuts and bruises.

That evening as Father Cavanagh was saying Grace before their meal of stirabout, he noticed the two boys with their marked faces. "You two," he said, pointing to the two fighters. "Over to the rectory."

With both young men before him in his kitchen, the priest said, "I warned ye. Here I am trying to feed a hundred starving children, and you want to maul each other. Tomorrow from dawn until sundown, you'll clean and polish every inch of the dormitories."

After a day of scrubbing floors and washing walls, Johnjoe and Tommy kept their hands off of each other, but it was an uneasy truce.

* * *

In his Dingle barracks, Captain Packenham received a letter from his commander in Dublin. He read it to Lieutenant Thomas:

Captain Packenham:
You have three weeks in which to find the murderer of Major Mahon. London is rife with rumors about an Irish uprising, and we must move fast to quell disorder.
General Penny

"Lieutenant, we have no leads at all. You mentioned a boy whose dog I killed."

"Johnjoe Kevane."

"And his name was listed in *The Freeman's Journal* as among the dead at Grosse Ile," said Captain Packenham.

"Yes, Captain."

"We have a copy of the paper here on my desk. Let's look at it again," Captain Packenham said. "Something has always troubled me about that list."

The two officers brought the paper to the window so the captain could read it more easily in the light. "See that last line: 'Scarce a fragment of those three thousand exiles now survives'. Maybe Kevane is one of the survivors returned to haunt us. You told me you saw a spark in the boy that could mean trouble."

"Yes, Captain. He was fearless and looked you square in the face when you cut his dog in two."

"Lieutenant, I have a feeling about this. I know you're wary of me putting Canon Long to the test, but we've got to push him more. He knows something."

"Yes, Captain. We also could go to see this Bishop Browne at Elphin to find out if he knows about any survivors. This is his list in *The Freeman's Journal*. He's Canon Long's superior and might nudge him to tell what he knows. These bishops are afraid of an uprising. If we could plant the seed that the canon is protecting a murderer, the bishop may help us pry information from Canon Long."

"An excellent idea, Lieutenant. We'll head off tomorrow morning."

Early the next day Lieutenant Thomas said, "Before we go to see Bishop Browne, Captain, let's check on the whereabouts of the boy's companion, Brother Leonard. I saw Canon Long out in his horse and buggy today, and I wondered if the two fugitives had come back without our knowing it."

"Good thinking. We'll walk down to the monastery."

Brother Gerald answered the Captain's knock. "Good morning, Officers."

"Lieutenant Thomas saw the canon with his horse and trap," said Packenham.

"Brother Leonard didn't return it."

"So Brother Leonard is not here, you say," said Captain Packenham.

"He is not, Sir," said Brother Gerald.

When the two officers left, Brother Gerald was pleased with himself. He had given nothing away, not telling the captain that Brother Leonard had been transferred to St. John's, Newfoundland, indeed had already left. The captain could find out that for himself.

Chapter 11

As the summer in St. Michael's wore on, the farmers all waited the development of the potato seedlings. They prayed that they would have potatoes this year. Sadly the blight struck for the third year in a row. As for himself, Johnjoe was happy in his schedule of work and writing.

Josie Mullins burst into the kitchen one afternoon where Johnjoe sat writing: "Sister, Sister, a band of tinkers is coming up the road from town."

"Well, invite them in for a meal."

First to enter were the children, dirty even for these times. Sister Clare knew that their parents hung back in wooden horse-drawn caravans to see if the coast was clear. The tinkers were afraid of the sheriff and the authorities who suspected them of thieving horses, pigs, and other livestock. "Tinkers" or "Travelers" was the name originally given to tinsmiths who traveled the countryside to repair pots and pans. They roamed the country in groups, sending their young children out to beg.

Sister Clare knew the origin of the tinkers was uncertain. Some thought Cromwell's armies drove them off the lands of Irish lords when he gave their land to Protestants. The Famine added to their displacement. Often mistakenly associated with the Roma or Gypsies, the tinkers were genetically pure Irish with red or blond hair and fair skin.

"Sit down, why don't you," said Sister Clare to the ragtag mob.

"Here's some stirabout to bring to your elders, but I want the pot back, mind."

A tinker in his twenties, dressed more neatly than the rest, told Sister Clare, "While these are eating, I'll repair any pots and pans that need it." The children spoke in their own language, *Shelta,* while they ate.

Sister Clare brought out frying pans and kettles, all of which the tinker youth repaired neatly. Something about the nun's manner evoked respect. She did not shy away from them.

"Tommy, go over to Father's kitchen and bring back any pots that need fixing; Johnjoe, give him a hand."

When the young tinker had mended all the pots and pans, Sister Clare made him sit down and eat his own stirabout.

"Lad, it's a wonder your people survive the terrible Famine," said Sister Clare, sitting across the table from the young man.

"Sometimes farmers give us their dying or dead horse. The people call us "knackers" for eating the meat. Most have nothing to do with us, treating us as thieves, but you haven't done that. You've been kind."

"These are hard times for all of us, travelers or no. You can always call in when you need a meal. If we can feed you, we will."

After the young man had finished eating, the nun told him to bring an empty pot from the caravan, which she would fill with stirabout for their journey. The youth did so and said to Sister Clare, "You've been generous to us, Miss. Thanks."

As the tinker left the school, Tommy Linnane was waiting outside and called him over. "A fine spring lamb is ready for the taking, caught in some brambles on the way to the river."

Though the sister had been good to him, the tinker knew he couldn't pass this up. Johnjoe was nowhere in sight, probably writing in that fool of a book, so Tommy had a clear field. Johnjoe had been searching for the lamb for hours, he and his dog driving the rest of the sheep near the road next to the woods.

The tinker drew a knife, and Tommy was excited for the kill as they spotted the lamb stuck in a maze of thorn bushes. But Johnjoe's dog found the lamb first as the tinker and Tommy were closing in, coming down from a hill a little above the brush.

Johnjoe's voice pierced the bleating of the sheep: "Cut that lamb and you'll have me to deal with." Armed only with a staff, Johnjoe ran toward them.

"We'll take you on, and make you fit for the knackers, too," shouted Tommy.

But the tinker saw only trouble and ran back to the caravans.

Tommy was left facing Johnjoe who said to him. "I bet it was you that led that thief here. You're worse than the tinkers. At least they have a reason for living the way they do. You're just Irish dung."

Tommy's face flared red, but he wanted no more beatings from Johnjoe. "I suppose now you'll run off and tell Father Cavanagh and Sister Clare."

"We'll see," said Johnjoe, giving the boy an unnecessary wallop across his shoulders with his staff.

As Johnjoe returned his diary to Sister Clare who was baking bread over a hot stove, he asked, "Sister, I'm wondering if you had time to read any of my book."

For a moment she didn't reply, but gathered herself leaning against the kitchen table. "I don't know how you've gone through what you have. You make all the suffering real. This is a powerful book entirely."

"Sister, I don't understand how a loving, compassionate Christ allows our people to endure so much pain."

She grabbed Johnjoe and hugged him. "I have no answer for you, but mind you finish this book. Now get out of my kitchen so I can make supper. One last thing, beware of Tommy. He means you no good."

Sister Clare realized that she knew more about Johnjoe than anyone else, but she kept his secrets to herself. He reminded her of her younger brother Cathal, who needed her guidance. She loved them both as a mother.

* * *

The Irish Famine, 1850 (oil on canvas) by George Frederic Watts (1817-1904) © Trustees of the Watts Gallery, Compton, Surrey, UK/ The Bridgeman Art Library

Bishop Browne of Elphin accepted Captain Packenham's request for an interview. He and Lieutenant Thomas rode north through the Slieve Mish Mountains, greenery all around them except for the black and gray rocks and far off the blue of Dingle Bay. They were miles from any other city, and the scenery was unchanged: broken-down cottages with weeds and bushes about to reclaim the land where people once lived.

When they had reached Bishop Browne's two-story brick residence, many starving people were waiting in front for food. Packenham bashed his way through the people to bang on the door. A rose garden stood beside the house and a vegetable garden in back.

Dressed in black, an elderly housekeeper opened the door and offered them tea. Bishop Browne received them in his study: a desk and three chairs, an oak kneeler below a crucifix of the same wood, and shelves of books from floor to ceiling. Four years into his office, the tall rugged-looking priest had been nicknamed the Dove of Elphin for his meek ways. No more. The Dove had become a Lion for his starving people.

Packenham began, "We've come to investigate the shooting of Major Mahon."

"Any man who shot Major Mahon deserves the blame of all honest men."

The captain went on: "Several of his parishioners claimed that Canon Long denounced him from the pulpit."

"And these men have come forward in person to face Canon Long," said the Bishop.

"No, Bishop. They're afraid."

"It's strange that with our little island bristling with dragoons like yourselves—more than you have in India—that people are afraid of a poor country priest."

"But Canon Long admitted to me that he and the major had exchanged violent words at the workhouse meeting the night he was murdered," said the captain.

"Violent words are not violent deeds," the bishop said as the captain's eye patch began to jump with a life of its own.

"Bishop, we suspect Canon Long and a brother, Brother Leonard, are protecting a youth whose name appears on your list of emigrants—Johnjoe Kevane," Captain Packenham said.

"Captain," said the Bishop. "Let me be sure I understand you.

First, you suspect Canon Long. Now you mention Brother Leonard and a young man. I don't know whom you are accusing."

"Bishop, we think this Kevane boy may have shot Major Mahon because when we raced after him, he and Brother Leonard ran and hid from us."

"But sure he was 3,000 miles away in Canada, that is, if he survived the coffin ship."

"He could have made his way back here for revenge," said the captain.

"This is the same Brother Leonard who has left the country to found a school in St. John's, Newfoundland," said the bishop.

"He told us he was bringing the boy to Tralee," Captain Packenham said.

"I have a letter from Brother Leonard's superior saying that Brother Leonard has left for Newfoundland," said the bishop.

"No one told us that. You have news of Kevane," the captain said.

"I know only that he was in one of Major Mahon's evicted families," the bishop said.

"Bishop, I'm very disappointed in your responses. I hoped you would force Canon Long to reveal what he knows of the murderer," the captain said.

"Captain Packenham, Lieutenant Thomas, my responsibility is to take care of my starving people, not to please you. Now, let us turn to a consideration of your work, every day tearing down the houses of the starving, scenes that would shame a Nero or Caligula. Secretary of the Treasury Trevelyan considers the Famine a 'mechanism for reducing the surplus population. The judgment of God sent the Irish a calamity to teach the Irish a lesson . . . .' You officers believe that starvation is God's means of reducing our population."

" I take no part in religion or politics," the captain said.

"I understand you're an avid reader of the Bible, Captain."

"Yes.'

"Perhaps you recall these verses from *Exodus* 22: 'You shall not wrong any widow or orphan. If ever you wrong them, I will surely hear their cry. My wrath will flare up, and I will kill you with the sword. . . .' And there are famished people outside my front door."

"They are not my duty."

"I wonder whose duty they are."

When Packenham remained silent, the bishop said, "I see, Captain. Just like Pontius Pilate who washed his hands of the blood of Christ."

Packenham reddened and his eye patch quivered, his nerves on edge.

Bishop Browne continued, "You put violent hands on Canon Long in his own rectory."

"He was concealing the murderer. He still is," said the captain.

"You shot a man in the Dingle workhouse," said the bishop.

"The man had a hammer and was menacing me," the captain said, "not that I need give any account of my actions to you. After Mahon's death even Queen Victoria said the Irish 'are a terrible people. . . .' And Lord Palmerston is correct when he says that Ireland is made up of 'ferocious, bloodthirsty villains who are forcing landlords to give up their estates.'"

"And this is the same Lord Palmerston who has sent nine coffin ships to Canada this year," said the bishop.

"I don't know, Bishop."

"Well, I do. It is the same man, Captain, an absentee landlord living in London sending Irish tenants to their deaths so he can graze sheep on their land. Mr. Adam Ferric, a member of the Legislative Council of Canada, wrote an open letter to Earl Grey, the British Colonial Secretary, excoriating Mahon and Palmerston. I'll take the liberty of reading it to you: 'Hordes of half-naked starving paupers including aging, infirm, vagrants and beggars, had been shipped off to this young and thinly populated country without regard to humanity or even to common decency. They were given promises of clothes, food and money and that an agent would pay from two to five pounds to each family, according to size, on arrival at Quebec; when they arrived, no agent could be found, and they were thrown on the Government and private charity. Twice as many passengers as the ship should hold were 'huddled together between decks', there was too little food and water and conditions were 'as bad as the slave trade.' Calling the Famine a calamity of God, an act of His Providence, relieves England of the responsibility of feeding Ireland's starving population," said the bishop.

"We're soldiers, Bishop," said Captain Packenham.

"And you are Christians," the bishop said.

As the two officers left the rectory, Lieutenant Thomas said, "The bishop is better informed than we about the condition of our exiles."

"That's nothing to do with us," Packenham replied. "Our task is to uphold the law." But enforcing the law had its own price for Packenham. Headaches seared him, whether from his obsession with the murderer or from seeing with only one eye.

Chapter 12

BRIDGET O'DONNEL AND CHILDREN.

"The Sketch of a Woman and Children represents Bridget O'Donnell. Her story is briefly this: — ' . . .we were put out last November; we owed some rent. I was at this time lying in fever . . . they commenced knocking down the house, and had half of it knocked down when two neighbours, women, Nell Spellesley and Kate How, carried me out . . . I was carried into a cabin, and lay there for eight days, when I had the creature (the child) born dead. I lay for three weeks after that. The whole of my family got the fever, and one boy thirteen years old died with want and with hunger while we were lying sick.'"

Illustrated London News, December 22, 1849

From Steve Taylor's Website Views of the Famine

http://adminstaff.vassar.edu/sttaylor/FAMINE/

Johnjoe took his diary out with him those days when he was minding the sheep, sitting on a boulder in the pasture or on stacks of hay near the barn. In the evenings when he had returned it to her care, Sister Clare again took up the diary, coming close to the point where Johnjoe had finished writing.

* * *

As Father Cavanagh and Johnjoe escorted the body of another fever victim to the cemetery, Gray rode up to harass them again: "Well, Cavanagh, have you read Prime Minister Russell's latest pronouncement? 'We here in England have done too much for the Irish and lost the election for doing so.'"

"Perhaps Russell should cross the sea and see what things are like here," said the priest.

"And Treasurer Trevelyan has declared he will buy no more corn from America and will continue exports of food from Ireland. He sees the Famine as I do, 'a direct stroke of an all-wise and all-merciful providence'. He views you Catholics as 'a nation of beggars', ruled by 'indolence and disorder', like the young tinker there who pulled me from my horse."

"But Mr. Gray, Sir," Johnjoe said. "I was relieving your horse of the burden of your corpulence. You're making it sway back."

"Mr. Gray, you should hold your tongue, and save yourself from further embarrassment," said Father Cavanagh.

Turning red in the face, Gray said, "You tinker, I suppose you have a name."

"Johnjoe Kevane."

"I will get you some day," Gray threatened.

* * *

Like Johnjoe, Sister Clare debated how a loving, compassionate Christ could allow so much suffering and death in her country. Living on a farm outside Dublin, her own family was healthy, thank God. Sister Catherine McAuley, founder of the Sisters of Mercy, drew her to the order because the "walking nuns," as they were called, worked with and among the people, teaching children and feeding the poor in contrast to contemplative nuns who huddled in their convents and prayed. Johnjoe's questions troubled her, but instead of thinking deeply about them, Sister Clare taught and fed those in her care. Her prayer was work.

One evening at dusk as Johnjoe and the dog were bringing in the flock, four tinkers jumped up from a ditch and knocked him to the ground. "I've got him," one tinker yelled, and hit him on the head with a rock the size of a teapot.

"Oh, Jesus," Johnjoe yelled. His dog danced around barking as it tried to keep the tinkers away. What they really were after was sheep. With long knives, they slashed the throats of two sheep while the rest of the herd scattered. A gunshot cut through the evening. Father Cavanagh had heard the yelling and fired a shot in the air at the edge of the field.

Taking the two dead lambs, the tinkers headed for the woods on the east side of the farm, the dog still chasing them. A tinker ran over to Johnjoe for one last kick when he bounced up and caught the thief around the ankles with the crook of his staff. "You dirty bastard," Johnjoe shouted. The boy tripped and fell face-forward in the grass. Johnjoe jumped on him and held him down. Father Cavanagh ran up, shouting "Johnjoe, you've got blood all over your head. "

"I'm just stunned is all. The dog kept them off me."

"Dirty tinkers," Father Cavanagh said. "We'll haul this one to the sheriff. All they have to do is ask for food, and we'd give it to them. But they'd rather steal it. Two fine ewes."

When Johnjoe got up shakily, he pulled the robber by his hair, his face covered with blood, mud, and sheep dung. It wasn't a tinker at all, but Tommy Linnane. "You dirty *sleveen bollix*" (useless creep), Johnjoe screamed.

Johnjoe pummeled him, drawing blood, until Father Cavanagh stopped him. "Johnjoe, you'll kill the devil." He then turned to Tommy. "You ingrate. You would do this to those who fed you and gave you a home. Get out of here. You're not even worth taking to the sheriff. Sure you don't even care for your own sisters." He kicked the boy in the backside.

Tommy turned to Johnjoe and shouted, "I'll get you. You'll be sorry you ever saw me."

"I'm sorry already," Johnjoe said.

When the priest and Johnjoe got back to St. Michael's, Sister Clare cleaned the young man's head wound. Johnjoe said, "We'll have to lock the sheep in the barn or the tinkers will be after more of them. Father, perhaps your friend could give us another border collie. Two dogs working together would be easier for us to keep the sheep together."

"A good idea," said Father Cavanagh. "I'll see Jim Fogarty tomorrow for another pup."

Tommy Linnane was not to be scoffed at. For a few days he lived rough in the forest. But he had a plan for getting back at Johnjoe. With his dog, Johnjoe often drove the sheep to the river. Tommy would get a knife, hide in the bushes, and kill him.

He knew that Johnjoe's parents had died aboard ship in Canada and that the youth was listed in the bishop's letter in the newspaper as among those evicted by Major Mahon. A Christian Brother brought him to Listowel with the Mullins girls. Some connection linked Johnjoe and Major Mahon, but Tommy wasn't seeing it. Tommy walked to the town center and guessed that his best option would be the workhouse, where at least they would feed him.

* * *

During these summer months, Johnjoe began to fall in love with Mary Mullins who was growing into a beauty. Her long raven hair grew back and light freckles dusted her face, a contrast to her blue eyes. One afternoon an hour before supper, Johnjoe asked her if she would like a walk toward town. She consented.

No one was on the road but the two youngsters. Skylarks and thrushes wheeled overhead against an azure sky. Johnjoe worked up his courage and reached for Mary's hand. She didn't resist. He described to her his life in Ballyristeen and the tumbling of the family home.

"Your Ma and Da were sick before you left Ireland," Mary said.

"No. They took sick only at the end of the voyage."

"It must have been terrible lonely for you when you lost them."

"Thank God I had people who were kind to me like the mistress on ship; Mr. Whyte, a journalist; and Father Moylan."

"Josie, Nellie, and I were blessed that Brother Leonard and you came into our lives. I don't know where we'd be otherwise."

As they neared St. Michael's on their return home, Johnjoe looked to see if anyone was watching. When he saw no one, he risked a kiss. Mary was receptive, giving him hope for the future.

* * *

In June Bewley brought his load of cornmeal and rice to St. Michael's. The Quakers had learned that rice added to the soup made it more substantial. He came with two loads, the second for the Listowel workhouse. He asked Johnjoe if he would help unload at the workhouse, and the young man agreed.

When they came to the workhouse with its imposing stonewalls, Bewley and Johnjoe had to pass by men and boys breaking stones in the courtyard, Tommy Linnane among them. As Johnjoe walked by carrying a sack of cornmeal with both hands, Tommy spat in his face.

"You lout," said Bewley, and then took out his own handkerchief to clean Johnjoe's face.

"He's a bloody informer who got me in trouble with Father Cavanagh," Tommy said.

"I don't believe you," said Mr. Bewley. "I'll bet you're good at finding your own trouble."

Johnjoe wanted to punch Tommy, but he respected Mr. Bewley and the Quaker views on pacifism. On the ride back to St. Michael's, Bewley said, "I admire your restraint in not fighting back."

After seeing Mr. Bewley all these months, Johnjoe could see that his relief work was wearing him down. He was running his own tea and coffee shops in Dublin, and he was the chairman of the relief committee. The Quakers were doers, making surveys of the needs of the country, and then maintaining soup kitchens all over Ireland.

When Johnjoe mentioned how careworn Mr. Bewley was growing, Father Cavanagh agreed, "The poor man is killing himself for the poor. The Quakers keep exact records and are wise and kind. They publish letters and tracts and even appear before Parliament to try to get Prime Minister Russell and Treasurer Trevelyan to help us. They trust in their own goodness and have no fear of the government in London."

* * *

A few days after Captain Packenham and Lieutenant Thomas had visited him, Bishop Browne summoned Canon Long from Dingle to his residence. This was a ride of more than two hours through the Slieve Mish Mountains, the blue waters of Dingle Bay on his right, the boulder-strewn mountains on his left. As he approached the bishop's rectory, the priest had to make a path through the beggars crowding around the front door hoping for a meal.

The priest sat in the bishop's parlor, each of them enjoying a cup of tea.

"Danny," said the bishop, "we've known each other for years.

I gave those dragoons who interrogated me short shrift, but I have to know if their story has any truth. You know this boy, Johnjoe Kevane."

"I do, Bishop."

"Did he shoot the major?"

"Bishop, I can't reply to you because of the Seal of Confession."

"Good God, I didn't realize. Danny, you've done well. Keep the Seal of Confession. I upbraided Packenham for roughing you up. He's a strange one, cold as a stone. I wonder how did he lose his eye?"

"In the Punjab in India, Bishop. A Sikh soldier slashed it out before Packenham killed him. He keeps the blade still as a souvenir, he's never without it."

"Danny, we will never be rid of these English, starving our people and sending them away to die."

"There are no signs of hope, Bishop. They have hardened their hearts against us."

Fortified by his tea, Canon Long set out for Dingle, but not before giving away all the money he had to the beggars at the bishop's door.

Chapter 13

Every few days Johnjoe took Mary out for a walk before supper, a stroll of more than a mile with oak trees in full leaf on both sides of the road. They would go to the edge of Listowel and head back. One afternoon, Josie Mullins, at eleven the second of the three sisters, came from behind the school building and saw the two holding hands, blurting out, "I'll bet you two are going to get married."

Mary blushed, making her look even more beautiful, her flame-red cheeks contrasting with her black hair.

"No," Mary replied. "We're friends is all."

Johnjoe replied, "Maybe we'll get married later."

Still crimson, Mary reproved him. "Don't be so sure of yourself, Johnjoe Kevane."

Johnjoe's feelings were hurt. To make matters worse, because Josie was walking into St. Michael's with them, he didn't get to kiss Mary.

Two afternoons later Johnjoe and Mary were walking. Part way on the road into town, Johnjoe took Mary into his arms for a long passionate kiss. He could feel her breasts plumping out the top of her calico dress, and he wanted to feel them. Sensing his intention, Mary pulled back from him and just in time too because Father Cavanagh in his horse and trap came around a bend. He said to the couple, "Holding hands and the odd kiss are fine things, but mind you don't go too far. You'll have time enough for that."

"Yes, Father," they replied in unison, their faces bright red.

"Go on and finish your walk. It's better than riding with an old man in his trap."

As they walked back to St. Michael's, Johnjoe thought the only way he could get his hands on Mary was by marrying her—if then.

* * *

Bishop Browne from Elphin was on a mission. The bishop showed up unannounced at Father Cavanagh's door.

"Good God, Bishop, this is a surprise."

"Yes, Patrick, and what a sad journey through a starving people making their way to the workhouse. A disaster."

"Bishop, I'm feeding a hundred children across the road in the school, thanks to the Quakers."

"Patrick, on top of all this I was questioned by a Captain Packenham and the dragoons hunting for Johnjoe Kevane. You know the lad."

"Bishop, he's here, a wonderful young man, but it would be better if I have him speak for himself."

Father Cavanagh called Johnjoe from the barn. He left his boots outside the kitchen door.

Johnjoe was not awed by the bishop who said, "Now, lad, the truth. You shot the major."

After giving an inquiring glance at Father Cavanagh who nodded affirmatively, Johnjoe answered, "Yes."

"What in the name of God is wrong with you, to kill another man?"

"Bishop, he murdered hundreds, including me Ma and Da."

"The Fifth Commandment says 'Thou shalt not kill.'"

"Bishop, I confessed my sin, and I'm doing penance."

"Well, at least that's something."

"Bishop, I would like to tell you my story if you would stop haranguing me."

"Johnjoe, this is the bishop," interposed Father Cavanagh.

"No, Patrick, let's hear what he has to say. You didn't have to kill him."

"And let him kill hundreds more of us, Bishop. You did nothing to stop him."

"Johnjoe," Father Cavanagh hastened to intervene. "You're being too bold altogether."

"Patrick, we'll hear his story out."

"One morning at the end of our voyage as our ship lay in quarantine outside Grosse Ile, me Ma and Da woke with the fever, their faces swollen and black as night. Me Ma pushed me from the berth to save me, and I hovered by watching them die. Father Moylan gave them the last rites and then rowed me to shore. I stood and watched my parents harpooned by two sailors on one lance to pull them from the hold, naked and bloody. They were dumped into a cart on shore and hauled away to a mass grave on the western end of the island—over 5000 of us in that hole. Bishop, I was afraid to kiss them goodbye, but did it anyway."

"Johnjoe, the doctor cleared you of fever."

"Yes, Bishop, he examined my tongue and passed me. But really I wanted to die. Bodies were stacked on shore like firewood, and some poor frenzied people ran to the woods and were buried where they fell."

As the bishop listened to Johnjoe, he grew quiet and pensive, saddened by Johnjoe's tale. "I understand why you shot the man, lad, but I wish you hadn't."

"I don't deserve to hang."

"Yes, Johnjoe, you're right. But you have to be smart too. I know you're headstrong and courageous. Consider this. Start using the English word for Kevane, "Kavanagh," and get a fresh beginning for yourself as "John Kavanagh" working with the Quakers in Galway. From now on to the world, you're John Kavanagh. Patrick might get Mr. Bewley to take you on. Perhaps this is a way to compromise with your principles and avoid the hangman."

"Bishop, you've been kind to me. I'll do as you say."

The bishop liked Johnjoe and felt protective toward him.

"Johnjoe, one thing more. A group called Young Irelanders led by William O'Brien, Thomas Meagher, John Mitchel, Charles Gavan Duffy, and others is calling for revolt. They've gone beyond seeking to repeal the Act of Union. They want bloody uprising in Ireland as there is in France right now, but they've no chance. Starving men can't fight. The English hold all the cards in men and weaponry. Stay clear of them, mind, or else you'll call attention to yourself."

Before Johnjoe left to return to work, the bishop gave him his blessing and warned, "Be careful now, lad. Ireland has become dangerous for you."

The two priests finished their home brew. "This is a fine young man, Patrick, that you're helping, perhaps even a great one. If he goes to Galway and any bit of trouble arises, I want to know about it immediately. Even in our benighted country, a bishop can do some things. Here's twenty-five pounds to use as you like. You're doing great work here. Even the Quakers praise you, and they don't speak highly of anyone who doesn't deserve it."

Father Cavanagh thanked the bishop.

Chapter 14

After speaking with the Bishop Browne at St. Michael's, fresh memories of the voyage started Johnjoe writing again in his diary.

When in June Bewley brought his next load of corn and rice to the school, Father Cavanagh pulled him into his spartan parlor for a chat. Only a large wooden crucifix and picture of the Blessed Virgin Mary adorned the walls.

"Joseph, tell me about your model farm."

"It's going swimmingly, Father. We hired a Dr. Bewley from England as superintendent; he has the same name as I but no relation. He's investigated modern agricultural methods in England. He's built a large house with a stone fence running alongside the road, a piggery for 110 hogs, a stable for eighteen horses, a yard for 126 cows, and a granary of 130 barrels. We grow oats, barley, mangel, turnips, and rape. We've even diverted a stream for power and threshing machines. We're training dozens of new farmers in recent agricultural advances. Even the Scots Presbyterians, very stingy with praise, laud our efforts in encouraging strangers to come among the Irish and teach them how to cultivate the land."

"Joseph, a great favor. I would like you to take on another farmer trainee."

"Father, I hate to deny you, but we're full up with 240 young farmers. Right now we have a terrible crisis in Skibbereen. We need all the help we can get there, even for a few days, but it's dangerous, the most infected part of Ireland with the fever. We need workers for the soup kitchen there. After that we might be able to use a man at the Claddagh with the fisheries, someone with experience aboard ship who speaks Irish."

"My man has sailed to Canada and back. He also may have fished in Dingle Bay. I think you'll find him most suitable: Johnjoe Kevane."

"Father, I've had my eye on him for months, but you would miss him here yourself."

"Yes, Joseph, but I can have him train two of the younger boys, say, in a few weeks."

When Father Cavanagh explained Mr. Bewley's proposal to Johnjoe, the young man agreed: "I promised to serve the poor for two months as penance for my sin, and I'll go to Skibbereen as John Kavanagh, what the bishop suggested. The only drawback is that I'll be leaving Mary. We've become very close."

"Sure I noticed you playing patty-fingers on your walk. But this way you can stay clear of the dragoons and return later. Even the dragoons will be in no great hurry to visit Skibbereen because of all the death and disease there. Tell Sister Clare and the Mullins girls, but no one else, mind."

* * *

Captain Packenham's headaches were getting worse, whether from the pursuit of his murderer or the stress on his one good eye, denying him even the one pleasure he had of reading his Bible. Forced to cut back on his Bible study, during the day he often had to lie down with his eyes closed on his cot in the barracks, galling to him because his men could see his weakness. Petrified that he might lose the sight of his one good eye, he feared that his disability might cost him his command, a fate intolerable to him. He thought of blind Oedipus stumbling over the countryside weeping for his children. For over

106

two years he had been pursuing this murderer Kevane and never gotten any closer to him than that first morning after the shooting when he had met the killer and Brother Leonard on Conor Pass. He replayed that scene over and over in his mind, the boy's quietness and civility. He thought back to all the places he had hunted his prey: Dingle, Castlegregory, and Camp, Tralee, and Listowel. At every stop Catholic priests and brothers had lied to him, protecting a murderer. He couldn't understand why. From his Bible he found no consolation. He was bone-tired of the hunt, but it was the only thing he knew to do.

Packenham's Pursuit of Johnjoe

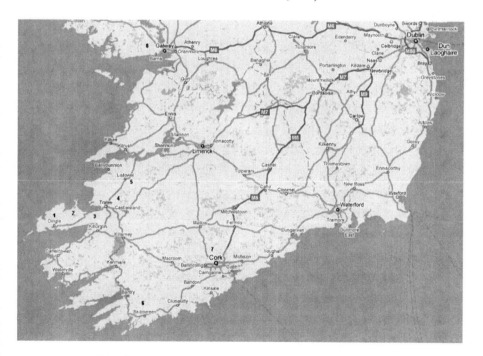

1. Dingle
2. Castlegregory
3. Camp
4. Tralee

More and more he began to fear for himself, worried that he was losing his mind and his humanity in searching for this villain. Bishop Browne had touched a nerve in him. He didn't want to become Pontius Pilate washing his hands of Christ's blood. The thought haunted him.

* * *

It was time for Johnjoe to leave St. Michael's, trying to keep one step ahead of Packenham. He dreaded saying goodbye to the Mullins girls, especially Mary whom he loved. She was angry at his going. "Johnjoe, nothing can be so important that you have to leave us. Some older brother you are."

"Mary, I love you. Someday I'll tell you my story, but I must leave to save my life. Trust me that I'll return to you." Johnjoe kissed her passionately in full view of Josie and Nellie, Sister Clare and Father Cavanagh, but he didn't care who saw.

Surprised, Mary shoved him away. "What kind of a woman do you think I am?"

"My woman," he said.

Turning red, Mary said, "You've grown too bold altogether. Don't be so sure of yourself." She then went upstairs and cried into her knitting.

The priest gave him a few pounds for his journey, and Johnjoe and Bewley set out for Skibbereen.

Chapter 15

Contemporary view of the battle at the Warhouse, Ballingarry, July 29, 1848. http://www.ballingarry.net/warhouse/guide.html

For months rumors of an Irish rebellion had filled the country. Captain Packenham reasoned that the murderer of Major Mahon might be involved in plans for an uprising in Ireland. The hunt for the fugitive would continue among the rebels. The "white-boys," so called because they wore white shirts, and the "ribbon men," whose badge was two pieces of green and red, and other secret agrarian societies, were terrorizing the countryside, threatening landlords and farmers who cooperated with them. Another group, United Irishmen, talked of armed rebellion. But a starving people couldn't mount a revolution.

As Bishop Browne had warned Johnjoe, an Irish insurgency of a sort broke out in Ballingarry, County Tipperary, where a group of Young Irelanders surrounded the local police in a farmhouse. Johnjoe heeded the bishop's advice and stayed miles away from the trouble.

William Smith O'Brien, Young Ireland leader, had held rallies in towns in the country and worked up an enthusiastic following. On Saturday, July 29, a contingent of police approached Ballingarry and were routed by 200 men and women led by O'Brien. The police barricaded themselves into a two-story stone farmhouse occupied by the Widow McCormack's children. She intervened with the police and with O'Brien for the release of her youngsters.

Looking for any sign of Kevane, Captain Packenham and his dragoons raced to the scene, ready to be doing something more exciting than knocking down the cottages of poor tenants. In April of 1848, the British Parliament had passed the Treason Felony Act mandating exile for fourteen years as punishment for any rebellion. Overwhelmed by paranoia, the British sent 10,000 more dragoons to Dublin, anxious to preserve their breadbasket of food from Ireland.

Outside Mrs. McCormack's home, shots were fired, and Packenham's dragoons arrived. They chased the rebels, Packenham killing one man with his musket and wounding another.

"We've got them on the run," Packenham yelled when a boy, red-haired and wild-eyed, erupted from a ditch and thrust a pitchfork into his face.

"Good God, I'm blinded," the captain screamed as blood gushed from his forehead into his good eye, the patch torn from his face. "Oh, anything but this. 'My God, my rock of refuge, my shield, the

110

horn of my salvation, my stronghold. Praise be the Lord I exclaim, and I am safe from my enemies.'"

Lieutenant Thomas raced over and with a handkerchief wiped the blood from the captain's face, revealing the scar and his empty eye socket. Once he could see, Packenham screamed, "Show me the bastard."

"There he is, Captain," the lieutenant pointed to a boy scrambling across a field. With his horse, Packenham ran the boy down and hacked at him with his kirpan, knocking him bleeding to the ground.

"Take away my one good eye, would you," the captain yelled as he continued to butcher the boy's dead body.

Packenham pulled out his musket and shot the boy as if to make him more dead.

The lieutenant rode over and said, "Patrick, stop. He's gone. We've caught some prisoners in the barn. You may want to interrogate them."

In a barn of faded red, three shivering young boys were tied to posts. Packenham stormed in and screamed at them: "I want Kevane, the murderer of Major Mahon."

The boldest of the three prisoners, a farmer's son, answered: "We know of no Kevane, Captain. He mustn't be from these parts."

Packenham, conscious of his empty eye, smashed the boy with his riding crop across the face: "You're hiding him just like those lying clergy."

"Captain, we have no Kevane among us."

When the boy protested further, Packenham said, "A good pitch capping will loosen your tongues. I want Kevane. Lieutenant, have one of the men boil some tar."

Lieutenant Thomas said to Packenham, "These are just three young boys, Captain. The fight is gone out of them. They know nothing of Kevane. Rather than work up the hatred of the locals, we should march them off to jail where they can be sentenced to exile. More importantly, we must look to your wound."

For once Packenham agreed with his lieutenant; and while his men took the three captives to jail, the captain found a doctor in the village to stitch up the cuts on his forehead and to make him a new eye patch, his nakedness once more covered. But he had still failed to capture his prey.

The Irish mutiny ended in ignominy, a few Irish farmers put to rout by the dragoons, the resistance so feared by the English. But though the uprising failed, it sowed in the Irish the seeds of future rebellion.

As farcical and ineffective as the insurrection was, it stirred up great hate in England. Father Cavanagh read with horror an article reprinted from *The London Spectator:* "How to Roast an Irish Patriot."

"Pick out a young one; speakers or editors are very good. Tie the arms behind the back, or close to the sides, but not too tight or the patriot will be prevented from moving, and the ribs will not be done. Skewer down to the pile. You will want a strong, steady fire. Dry pine makes a very good blaze. When the fire gets low, throw in a little oil or fat. When nearly done, a little gunpowder thrown in will make the patriot skip: some cooks consider this important."

The priest could only think of Johnjoe and shudder.

* * *

As Joseph Bewley and Johnjoe were headed south from Listowel with their wagonload of corn and rice for Skibbereen, they came to the village of Killarney and the Gap of Dunloe, which knifes through the Purple Mountains, the highest mountain range in Ireland. A stream runs alongside the narrow road into Lake Leane.

The road had sharp winding turns, so travelers often had to pull off the road allowing room for those coming against them. Heading towards Bewley and Johnjoe was a troop of scarlet-jacketed dragoons. Johnjoe braced himself to bolt from the wagon if Packenham were among them. When the soldiers had come closer, Johnjoe could see that Packenham was not with them. Bewley pulled their wagon off to the side of the road.

"Thank you, Sir. I can see by your garb that you're a Quaker. I'm Captain Redmond, just back from putting down a rebellion at Ballingarry. The rebels attempted to co-opt the French in their cause, but London warned them off. I wish more of the Irish shared your pacifist views."

"No loss of life, I hope, Captain," Bewley said.

"Not on our side, but Captain Packenham killed two young farmers who attacked him."

Johnjoe grimaced.

"And the other rebels," Bewley said.

"Hauled off to jail. They'll probably face charges of treason and be exiled to Australia. Certainly the leaders Meagher and O'Brien."

Johnjoe remained silent during this exchange until the captain addressed him. "Young man, I suppose you are a Quaker."

"No Sir. I'm accompanying Mr. Bewley to bring a load of corn and rice to the workhouse in Skibbereen."

"God knows they need it," the captain said. "It's the worst place for starvation and fever in Ireland. You're riding into hell. Take care, mind."

"Thanks, Captain. We'll do what we can," replied Bewley.

The dragoons rode past them, and Bewley and his helper journeyed on. Bewley said to Johnjoe, "The name "Packenham" is familiar to me and gave you a start."

"Yes, he's been hunting me for months. I would rather not tell you why."

"Then don't. Father Cavanagh recommended you, and I've seen nothing but hard work and goodness in you. Besides, I've seen cruelty from the dragoons with pitch capping and half-hanging, though these men here seemed friendly enough."

"Mr. Bewley, you're right."

"Also, your Pope has come out in opposition to any rebellion, and the Irish bishops will have to obey."

"But the Pope doesn't know what life is like on the ground here."

"Yes, Johnjoe, but even if I weren't a pacifist, I can see no good coming from an uprising. Famished men can't fight. My advice is to stay clear of the rebels. As is their way, the English will use this rebellion against us and punish the Young Irelanders severely. You can do more good for our people doing exactly what you're doing—helping to feed and care for the starving."

DESTITUTION IN IRELAND. — FAILURE OF THE POTATO CROP

"**Insurrection and rebellion would only lead to an aggravation of misery, the contemplation of which is sufficiently appalling to induce the right minded and humane to shrink from the consequences of recommending, even in the remotest contingency, any appeal to arms, unless, indeed, it were to invite the extirpation of the race as the only remedy against the destitution of which they are the unhappy victims.**"

Pictorial Times, August 22, 1846

From Steve Taylor's Website Views of the Famine

http://adminstaff.vassar.edu/sttaylor/FAMINE/

Bewley told Johnjoe about Asenath Nicholson, an American widow who had volunteered to work for a time at his soup kitchen in Dublin. "She's done wonders. In Dublin she met a crippled woman with two little children on the street. She nursed the woman and her children back to health, and helped the lady get a job as a seamstress."

"I wonder how she gets money for her charities," Johnjoe said.

"From friends in America and from us. Once we saw her good deeds, we were happy to advance her money because we knew it would be used well. She wrote a book, *Ireland's Welcome to the Stranger or Excursions through Ireland in 1844 and 1845*, and donated the royalties to Famine relief."

"On the political front," Bewley explained, "Daniel O'Connell, our greatest statesman, pleaded with Parliament to halt exports of food from Ireland and asked for additional aid to set up relief stations in all parts of Ireland. London rejected the proposal out of hand."

Lough Leane was on their left with rocks and boulders tumbled down from McGillycuddy Reeks, also called "The Black Stacks," formed from glacial carved sandstone stretching slightly over twelve miles. Though the scenery was beautiful, the two travelers knew that starvation and death loomed ahead.

Bewley told Johnjoe that the area of West Cork had lost almost half its population during the Famine years. The two men passed the ruins of Kilcoe Castle, near which the locals mined copper. Farther south on a desolate stretch of road, they came upon a young woman screaming on the road, a terrified child by her side. Two men were attempting to steal a small sack of cornmeal that the mother had just bought from a farmer.

Jumping down from the back of the wagon, Johnjoe waded into the two men who were wielding cudgels. With his fists he knocked loose a club from one thief and swung it at the other. "For shame," Johnjoe yelled, "robbing a mother and child."

"Mind your own affairs," one man screamed, "or we'll make mincemeat of you and your Quaker friend and leave you dead on the road."

Johnjoe used club against cudgel while the unarmed thief tried to haul him off. Bewley moved the mother and child away from the fight when Johnjoe thumped the first man so hard on his arms and chest that he dropped the weapon. As the other robber lifted a rock to strike Johnjoe on the head, Bewley knocked the rock to the ground and held the man's arms. Johnjoe was about to rain on more blows when Bewley stopped him.

"That's enough, lad. They're beaten."

The mother and little girl were shaken but unhurt. "Missus, climb aboard the wagon," Bewley told the woman.

"Don't take us to the sheriff," one of the thieves pleaded. "He'll hang us. We've got families to feed."

"All right then so," the Quaker said. "I know you're starving but have some decency."

Bewley took five shillings from his pocket and gave them to the men. "Take this and buy food for your families, no drink, mind."

Grateful, the men hobbled away.

"You're hurt, Johnjoe," Bewley said.

"Just some bruises that will heal. I know you Quakers believe in pacifism, but I had to fight them," Johnjoe said.

"Of course," Bewley responded. "They gave you no choice. You rescued the mother and child."

Johnjoe said, "You've saved more than one life today, Mr. Bewley."

The mother and child, Elizabeth and Nora Collins, had recovered from their ordeal with the would-be thieves, and rode along with Johnjoe in the back of the wagon.

"Thanks for your help," said Mrs. Collins to Johnjoe. "'Not everyone would take on two men to save a mother and child."

"'Tis nothing," Johnjoe replied.

"My husband is away in the British navy at Gibraltar, and it's only my little brother and the dogs to keep away robbers," she said.

When Bewley pulled the wagon in front of her whitewashed cottage, Elizabeth Collins invited them in for tea, but the two declined because they wanted to press on to Skibbereen, still some distance away. As Johnjoe helped the mother and daughter down from the wagon, Bewley handed the lady some shillings. "For food," he said.

"Bless you both," the mother said. "You've shown me Christ's goodness today."

* * *

A week after Johnjoe had slipped away with Bewley for Skibbereen, a fact unknown to Tommy Linnane, the villain came skulking around St. Michael's looking for a meal. Though Sister Clare had no use for him, she wouldn't deny him some stirabout and bread.

Tommy assumed Johnjoe would be out with the sheep. Before Tommy could interrogate the Mullins girls, whom Sister Clare had sworn to secrecy about Johnjoe's whereabouts, he had the ill fortune to run into Father Cavanagh in the dormitory.

"You're prowling about here again. We got rid of you," said Father Cavanaugh.

"Just here to see my sisters," Tommy said.

"I don't trust you, Tommy. Get out," said the priest.

One day in Listowel on a market day with only a scattering of shops open selling eggs, butter, and bread, Tommy spotted Mr. Gray astride his brown horse. "Excuse me, Sir, but that scoundrel who embarrassed you, Johnjoe Kevane, he may be in trouble with the law, I'm thinking. I saw the name Major Mahon written in a book he keeps, all very secret," Tommy said.

"Major Mahon was the landlord murdered near Dingle."

"Where Kevane is from," Tommy said. "I'm Tommy Linnane,

Sir. I used to live at St. Michael's until Kevane blackened my name. I stay at the workhouse now."

"The dragoons are scouring the country round for Mahon's killer, lad. I would love to see a noose around that criminal's neck. Nose around St. Michael's some more. Meantime I'll go to the authorities. You're a fine young man, and I'll give you a reward if you can report any more to me."

Tommy wanted Johnjoe dead, not only for thumping him several times, but he was in the way of his pursuit of Mary Mullins. She was smart and pretty and would make him a fine wife.

Gray wanted revenge. The Kevane wretch had caused him embarrassment twice, in front of Sheriff Costello and those bloody Quaker do-gooders. He would give a great deal to cause pain to Kevane, even hanging. Gray decided to make the trip of fifty miles to Dingle. He rode around Tralee, the bay on his right, and then headed south and west towards Dingle where the road ran alongside the Atlantic Ocean.

When Gray had reached Dingle, a villager directed him to the stone barracks of the dragoons just north of town. After knocking on the door and entering, a captain with a black eye patch met him. The black patch hypnotized Gray.

Recovering himself, Gray said, "Captain, I'm a landowner in Listowel and have ridden all the way here to give you information about a suspect you've been seeking—Johnjoe Kevane."

Packenham almost jumped at the man: "But you know it's the Kevane criminal."

"He told me his name. The snipe insulted me. He's a nasty piece of work, a mouthy young man. I can well believe he murdered the major. He's living with a bunch of other evictees at St. Michael's School under the care of a brazen priest, named Cavanagh. An informer can identify him, Tommy Linnane, living at the Listowel workhouse," Gray said. "If you take him with you, he'll help you root out the vermin."

Within half an hour Packenham had his dragoons ready for

the road. The captain was pulsating with energy, and Lieutenant Thomas knew he would have to stay close to his superior, afraid he would unleash immediate violence on the youth who had been his obsession these two years.

Gray was well pleased with himself. He had set his revenge in motion and could ride back to Listowel to savor the capture of his nemesis.

On their way through Listowel, the dragoons questioned Tommy Linnane at the workhouse, and he followed them to St. Michael's. Tommy, too, would enjoy this moment, his vengeance fulfilled.

When the dragoons had arrived at St. Michael's, Packenham bolted from his horse in anticipation. He banged on the door, which Sister Clare opened. She knew trouble when she saw it.

"I want Johnjoe Kevane," the captain barked.

She said, "I'll fetch Father Cavanagh from across the road."

"This delay will give them time to concoct more lies," Packenham told his men. He ordered them to search the building and the adjoining fields immediately. Two dragoons burst into the girls' dormitory cordoned off from the rest of the rooms. The girls shrieked at the invasion of their quarters by men armed with muskets and bayonets. When the soldiers asked about Johnjoe, the Mullins girls said nothing.

Father Cavanagh rushed from his rectory to face Packenham: "You've no right to come barging in here terrorizing little girls and children—dragoons or no."

"We have every right. We're hunting a murderer—Johnjoe Kevane," Packenham said.

"He's not here," the priest said. "A week ago he sailed off to help the brothers build a school for those whom you've driven from the country—in St. John's, Newfoundland."

"I don't trust you. You priests and religious specialize in lying. I'll have young Linnane here help us in our search."

"Ah, Tommy, so you're the informer. It's a role that suits you well," Father Cavanagh said.

Mary Mullins, her sisters, and the rest of the children heard this exchange.

"Kevane will hang," Packenham said.

Mary felt faint and started to cry.

"For any particular reason, or just your typical dragoon lawlessness," the priest said.

"Don't be insolent with me, Cavanagh. I don't care about your black dress and Roman dog collar. Kevane murdered Major Mahon."

"I'm sure you have proof and witnesses, Captain."

"He ran from us. When I get my hands on him, I'll make him confess," Packenham said.

"By your usual methods, I suppose, Captain, half-hanging and pitch capping."

"That's no concern of yours, Cavanagh, but I'll get him."

By this time Gray had overtaken the dragoons, anxious to find Kevane under arrest, but instead he found Packenham stomping around the school in a rage, his eye patch trembling. "It seems, Mr. Gray, that our criminal has escaped, left for St. John's, Newfoundland, according to Cavanagh here."

His hopes dashed, Gray unleashed his anger on Tommy. "You dirty tinker. You told me we'd find him here." Gray slashed Tommy across the face with his riding crop, drawing blood and raising red welts.

Father Cavanagh grabbed Gray's arm, snatched the leather crop, and hurled it into a field nearby, the second Gray had lost that way. "You're very predictable," Father Cavanagh said, "always a bully."

Tommy felt cheated by Johnjoe's absence, but his hate wouldn't allow him to give up. He'd bide his time with Gray and find some other way to get Johnjoe. Not for a second did he believe Johnjoe had sailed for Newfoundland.

Captain Packenham left Listowel more frustrated than ever. If he had to, he would chase Kevane to Newfoundland, a British colony 2000 miles and five weeks away by ship.

120

Chapter 16

A more immediate cause of starvation in Ireland was the export of food during a subsistence crisis, as documented for example in the work of Cormac O'Grada and Christine Kinealy. O'Grada explains *that 3,251,907 quarters (8 bushels = 1 quarter) of corn were exported from Ireland to Britain in 1845, along with 257,257 sheep.* He also provides evidence that *480,827 swine, and 186,483 oxen were shipped to Britain in 1846.* According to Kinealy, *9,992 calves and 4,000 horses and ponies were exported in 1847, and a total of 3 million live animals were exported from Ireland between 1846 and 1850. That is more than the number of people who emigrated or died during the famine years.* Kinealy's research reveals that *nearly 4,000 vessels carried food from the most famine-stricken parts of Ireland to the ports of Bristol, Glasgow, Liverpool, and London during 1847.* At the time her research was published, Kinealy documented that *1,336,220 gallons of grain-derived alcohol and 822,681 gallons of butter were exported to England during the first nine months of "Black '47."* Had these exports been redistributed by government command, thousands of Irish lives would have been saved.

"The potato failed from blight but the country was full of food, which was taken away from those who grew it, to be consumed by the expanding workforce of the industrial boom in England or by its army overseas."

http://www.wolfetonesofficialsite.com/famine.htm

Johnjoe knew that their destination, Skibbereen, which means "little boat harbor" in Irish, is on the southeast tip of Ireland, bisected by the River Ilen, which runs to the sea. It is part of West Cork, once a thriving area for growing potatoes. With the onset of the potato blight and the resulting Famine, Skibbereen became hell, the workhouse there having the most deaths of any in Ireland.

Bewley and Johnjoe passed dozens of people, both men and women, on the road smashing stones for outdoor relief, earning eight or nine shillings a day.

"To justify their actions," Bewley told Johnjoe, "the English endorse an economic policy of laissez-faire, to leave business alone, so they won't pay for seed and have us build roads to nowhere or make bridges where no water lies."

"Unless the potato blight relents, they'll have us all starved," Johnjoe answered. "These poor people on the road look ready to die, much less lift pick and shovel."

"Yes," Bewley said, "They're working on these useless projects to keep their families from death, instead of something with purpose for the country like planting seed and draining bog land for cultivation. Even many Irish Catholic farmers have profited from the Famine to indulge in land grabbing and other misdemeanors."

Just outside town, wagons of food guarded by dragoons headed for Cobh and English ships passed them by. Wagon after wagon of wheat, corn, and live pigs rolled past a starving people.

"Irish food for England," Johnjoe said.

THE FAMINE IN IRELAND.—FUNERAL AT SKIBBEREEN.—FROM A SKETCH BY MR. H. SMITH, CORK.—(SEE NEXT PAGE.)

"The ravages of disease at Skibbereen continue to be but too sadly confirmed. From a drawing made on the spot, we give a sketch of a scene of no unusual occurrence, as appears from the following extract of a letter from Skibbereen:—'Deaths here are daily increasing. Dr. Donovan and I are just this moment after returning from the village of South Reen, where we had to bury a body ourselves that was eleven days dead; and where do you think? In a kitchen garden. We had to dig the ground, or rather the hole, ourselves; no one would come near us, the smell was so intolerable. We are half dead from the work lately imposed on us.'"

From Steve Taylor's Website Views of the Famine

http://adminstaff.vassar.edu/sttaylor/FAMINE/

Approaching Skibbereen, the travelers found ten coffins made of deal, thin planks of pine, stacked against the side of a house. "Good God," Johnjoe said, "they can't have so many dead."

At the edge of town, Bewley and Johnjoe met two Oxford students, Dufferin and Boyle, who had wanted to see first-hand what conditions were in Skibbereen. They related a terrifying experience trying to give bread to the poor. Dufferin explained, "At first we sent the bread down to the door of our carriage, but the rush was so great, that the scheme became impracticable, and it only remained to throw it out of the window of our coach. One can never forget what followed: the fighting, the screaming, the swaying to and fro of the human mass, as it rushed in the direction of some morsel."

"At least you've done some good," Bewley said.

"We gave fifty pounds to Vicar Townsend, but Famine, typhus fever, and dysentery are sweeping away the whole population," Dufferin said. "When we return to London, we'll publish an account of what we've seen here. The world should know of this catastrophe."

"God bless," Bewley said.

Bewley and Johnjoe later reached the parsonage of Mr. Townsend, Church of England Vicar of Abbeystrewry Church, who welcomed them as a relief from the duties of death and burial. An old friend of Bewley's, Townsend was a tall man, stooped with the weight of the world on his shoulders.

"Vicar, I suppose you're able to manage," Bewley said.

"Things could hardly be worse. Nearly 200 have died in the Skibbereen workhouse in less than two months, and a hundred bodies were found dead on the streets and in cabins where they were gnawed by rats. 10,000 have died of a population of 100,000."

Inside a well-furnished dining room, they met Townsend's wife Mary, yards of purple linen lying by her feet. "I'm sewing shrouds for the dead," she explained. "Our two maidservants have died from the fever, and now it's impossible to give the dying the last rites and even to find coffins for them."

Ever polite even in such harrowing circumstances, Mr. Bewley asked Townsend about the workhouse to which they would deliver their load of cornmeal and rice. The vicar replied, "2800 there now in a building designed for 800. Three or four men lay in each bed, a man on the mend lying between two others raging with the fever. Mr. Bewley, I think God has forsaken us."

Bewley said, "I suppose there is no hope for the harvest."

"Look about you. The land is untilled because the government will give the farmers no seed so as not to compete with English farmers. The poor make relish cakes with animal blood, mushrooms, and watercress; eat turnip-cuttings or mangel-wurzel, cattle feed; and cook 'boxty,' rotten potatoes squeezed dry and baked."

On their way to the workhouse, the three men met a well-dressed man riding a bay horse. Townsend knew the man, Nicholas Cummins, a local magistrate. He appeared very shaken and told his story. "I came here armed with all the bread I could carry, and in the first house I visited six famished and ghastly skeletons, to all appearances dead, huddled in a corner on some filthy straw, their sole covering what seemed a ragged horsecloth, their wretched legs hanging about, naked below the knees. I approached with horror, and found by low moanings that they were still alive—they were in fever, four children, a woman, and what was a man. In a few minutes I was surrounded by at least 200 such phantoms, such frightful specters no words can describe, suffering either from Famine or from fever. Their demoniac yells are still ringing in my ears and their horrible images are fixed in my brain."

Riding alongside Cummins, the three men saw a mother, herself in fever, dragging out the corpse of her child, a girl about twelve, perfectly naked, and leave it on the road half covered with stones. "This is an outrage." Cummins said. "We live in a country dying before our eyes. I shall put this in a letter to the Duke of Wellington and have it printed in the *London Times*. We'll see if that will do any good."

Vicar Townsend wanted to show Bewley and Johnjoe some houses of the poor. They passed several cottages, which Townsend judged unsafe because of the danger of infection from the fever. Finally, he found one he deemed they could enter. Standing on the threshold, the three men peered into darkness. The floor was mud, the walls bare, without a stick of furniture because the family had pawned it for money to buy food. The mother was at the hearth heating some cornmeal, two naked children sitting without energy on some straw, and the husband rasping for breath from the fever. Bewley left some money with the mother.

A contemporary lithograph drawn by A. S. G. Stopford.

From Steve Taylor's Website Views of the Famine

http://adminstaff.vassar.edu/sttaylor/FAMINE/

In another cottage screaming and cursing greeted the visitors. On the floor were a father and his son groveling over the last potato. Johnjoe couldn't contain himself. Rushing over to the father, he screamed in his ear, "Leave off, you'd starve your own." Taking some shillings from his pocket, he shoved them into the man's hand.

In addition to the accounts of Townsend, Cummins, Dufferin and Boyle, government officials confirmed the abject state of Skibbereen. Major Parker, a relief inspector whom the Bewley, Townsend, and Johnjoe met on the road, described the horror to them. "A woman with a dead child in her arms was begging in the street yesterday, and the Guard of the Mail told me he saw a man and three dead children lying by the roadside. Nothing can exceed the deplorable state of this place."

Bewley and Johnjoe followed the example of the vicar who showed no fear in going into a cabin where the poor lay in fever. The *Times* accused the Irish of indifference towards the suffering, but the people were simply too weak to bury the bodies, and they feared infection from the dead as James Mahony, illustrator for *The London Times* writes, "the living cannot be prevailed to assist in the interments for fear of taking the fever."

The vicar led Bewley and Johnjoe to the graveyard close by. The ruins of an ancient Cistercian monastery, Abbeystrewsery, with broken walls and old tombstones, had become the cemetery. In one corner lay newly filled graves that shocked the visitors. Scantily clad bodies were thrown in one on top of the other with no coffins, only three inches of soil between them.

Johnjoe said, "I suppose there were no services for these poor souls."

"Sadly, none," answered Townsend. "Relatives don't even know where their own dead lie." In one corner, gravediggers dug a space two feet deep with bodies piled up, covered only by a bit of earth, a trench next to the corpses unfilled. Mr. Townsend barked to one of the workers, a gaunt young man in his twenties, "You haven't filled in the plot."

"We can't, Sir," said the man. "We've got six more bodies coming from the workhouse tonight."

As Townsend and his two guests were leaving, they stepped over some flattened earth with no mounds, a sign that no one was buried beneath. "Take your spades and dig here," Townsend said to the workers.

"We dare not, Sir," the young man said. "We dare not."

Exasperated, Townsend grabbed the spade from the man and began digging a short way—before he exposed a purple shroud.

Townsend explained to the two visitors that he was afraid of corruption from bodies buried so close to the surface during the warm summer months. "Some unfortunates dig a hole behind their cottage or in a garden for burial," Townsend said. "One poor man buried his wife in the garden and heard dogs howling that night. Very weak, he sent his daughter out to chase away the dogs, but they snapped at her. The next day one of the neighbors brought back the woman's head, saying 'the dog brought it home.'"

"At this moment, the funeral cart with its attendant came towards us; it stopped opposite the cottage; a deal coffin of a large size, in order to suit the dimensions of all persons, lay jolting at the top. . . . We learnt that the coffin was for a woman who lay dead in that house, and that four others of the same family lay sick of the fever, unable even to assist in removing the body of their relation."

Dufferin and Boyle, *Narrative of a Journey from Oxford to Skibbereen, 1847*

From Steve Taylor's Website Views of the Famine

http://adminstaff.vassar.edu/sttaylor/FAMINE/

As the bodies piled up, the gravediggers opened up pits in which the poor were dropped coffinless. Johnjoe told Bewley, "Bring the wagon of food to the workhouse where I'll be right along. I'm more fresh for digging than these fellows."

After an hour of hard digging, Johnjoe walked to the workhouse. Depressed and upset by what they had seen and heard, Johnjoe and Bewley found solace in work. They unloaded the cornmeal and rice at the Skibbereen workhouse, first boiling the corn maize into a soup under the direction of a Quaker woman, Mrs. Forster. Other Quaker women in their dress of brown and gray worked smoothly and efficiently, dispensing the soup in quarts to the ghosts waiting patiently in line for it.

THE CORK SOCIETY OF FRIENDS' SOUP HOUSE

"The Illustration shows a benevolent attempt to mitigate the suffering in the city of Cork, viz., the Society of Friends' Soup House. There are many similar establishments in operation through the county; but, we prefer the annexed because the idea originated with the Society of Friends."

Illustrated London News, January 16, 1847.

From Steve Taylor's Website Views of the Famine

http://adminstaff.vassar.edu/sttaylor/FAMINE/

Secretary of the Treasury Trevelyan had refused to send aid to Skibbereen because the town lacked an official committee to manage the program. And here were the Quakers not only buying the food, but cooking it in copper vats they had bought, and serving it too. Mrs. Forster gave Johnjoe explicit instructions: "Fill every carton full up. If people take a sip in front of you, top it off again."

Mrs. Forster seemed everywhere at once, checking the steaming vat and then shepherding the people into queues that flowed easily. Even Bewley took a backseat in the distribution of the soup, careful to follow Mrs. Forster's instructions.

A woman came in to the workhouse, pinch-faced and clutching to her breast a baby the color of chalk. Mrs. Forster found a seat for her and brought the soup over—"Two cartons for you, Deirdre," she said. "You're feeding two."

Docile and grateful, the people paid their one pence a quart to another Quaker woman, the money a way of preserving the dignity of the starving people, but not even covering the actual cost of the meal. When after some hours, the soup was beginning to run low, Mrs. Forster informed Bewley. Taking some money from his purse, Bewley said, "See if you can buy meat from the butcher to add to the corn maize and rice." Mrs. Foster bought some mutton, cooked it, and then added it to the soup.

A farmer who had been one of the first to be served came in at the end and complained to Mrs. Forster, "Sure the soup you're serving now is much better than I got."

A woman in line reproved him, "You're biting the hand that feeds you." Johnjoe thought of the wedding feast at Cana where Christ changed the water into good wine which was served last. Overhearing the dispute, Bewley told Mrs. Forster to give the man another carton of soup at no charge, even in this small matter exercising Quaker pacifism.

When they had finished serving all the people, Johnjoe and Bewley unloaded the rest of the corn and rice for the next day's meal.

Johnjoe watched how the Quaker women put the corn and rice into the vat adding water so the soup would cook over night. Standing on a small stepstool, Mrs. Forster used a long wooden pole to stir the mixture when Johnjoe relieved her and learned for himself.

Making himself useful by cleaning the kitchen, Johnjoe helped the Quakers, glad for his assistance. The weary, beaten-down poor with no energy or life saddened him. Into the workhouse came Captain Wynne, a middle-aged British relief officer desperate to talk. Cornering Bewley and Johnjoe, he bubbled with words. "I'm a man not easily moved, but I confess myself unmanned by the suffering I witness, especially among the women and little children scattered over the turnip fields, like a flock of famishing crows, devouring the raw turnips, mothers half-naked, shivering in the snow and sleet, whilst their children are screaming with hunger. I cannot stand this one more day. I'm going to serve in the Punjab in India, fighting rebels in the jungle."

The next day in the workhouse was like the first: hundreds of specters filing in for their soup, most from the day before, including the woman with the small baby whom Mrs. Forster served again. Johnjoe worked the whole day, ladling out the soup and cleaning the kitchen. It was dark when they finished. As they had done the night before, Bewley and Johnjoe stayed at a hotel in town, Bewley paying for a room for each of them, for which Johnjoe was grateful.

Chapter 17

BEGGING AT CLONAKILTY.

"I started from Cork for Skibbereen and saw little until we came to Clonakilty, where . . . the horrors of the poverty became visible, in the vast number of famished poor, who flocked around the coach to beg alms: amongst them was a woman carrying in her arms the corpse of a fine child, and making the most distressing appeal to the passengers for aid to enable her to purchase a coffin and bury her dear little baby. This horrible spectacle induced me to make some inquiry about her, when I learned from the people of the hotel that each day brings dozens of such applicants into the town." James Mahony.

Illustrated London News, February 13, 1847.

From Steve Taylor's website Views of the Famine

http://adminstaff.vassar.edu/sttaylor/FAMINE/

As Mr. Bewley and Johnjoe ate a late supper of broiled lamb in the hotel dining room, guilty that it was not stirabout, a group of businessmen nearby who had taken too much wine were scoffing at the idea that Skibbereen was short of coffins. Then one of the serving girls screamed as she passed a window. Caught in the light from the dining room, on the pavement below were two corpses with a blanket spread over them, a mother and an infant. A daughter of sixteen had brought the bodies and laid them there hoping to induce the hotel guests to donate money for their burial—as if she had heard the men inside the dining room talking dismissively of the need for coffins. The waiter rushed in and pulled the blinds, and gave a few six pence to the girl when Bewley and Johnjoe came out and added some shillings. Enough for a coffin.

As they prepared to leave next morning, Johnjoe said, "I can't stay here, Sir. The place has me depressed, nothing but sickness and death. The brothers run a soup kitchen in Cork. If you'd drop me off there, I'll volunteer to work for them. Perhaps they can give me a place to sleep."

"Fine, I understand, Johnjoe. You've been a help to me."

"Sir, I'm so discouraged."

"Yes. I feel the same, but at least we're saving some people. My real worry is that we're running out of provisions and money."

"But for you Quakers thousands more of us would have perished. I don't understand how a loving God could permit so much suffering."

"I have no answer for you, Johnjoe, but it's the right question. When I return from Dublin with another load of corn and rice, perhaps you'll accompany me to the Claddagh where you can help us with our fishing project there."

"I will indeed," said Johnjoe, "and it will keep me away from Captain Packenham."

It was less than an hour's ride to Cork where the Christian Brothers' school, St. Nessan's, was located at Sullivan's Quay in the shadow of the Anglican cathedral St. Finbarr's, the River Lee flowing below. The school was a square two-story brick building in the heart of the city. A Brother Clement, tall and handsome, prematurely gray, answered the door and told the two strangers that this was mealtime for the children. The man in charge, Brother John, was in the kitchen.

In a large, airy room, 200 boys and girls from five to twelve were busily eating corn meal porridge. The brothers had spread out two long tables the length of the room, an older child supervising every twenty or so kids. Because they could not all be served at one sitting, the boys and girls brought their spoons and bowls into the kitchen, and a new group took their place. Those who were finished went out to the courtyard to play.

When Brother John came to meet the two guests, his face flushed from leaning over the boiling vat of soup, the Quaker introduced himself, "Brother, I'm Joseph Bewley of The Society of Friends from Dublin, and I'm very impressed by what you're doing. This is organized but not intimidating. The children seem happy."

"Thanks, Mr. Bewley, but we've only enough corn for one meal a day, and we're getting more and more children from the outlying villages. For these we have cots in the dormitories. The city children return to their homes." Brother John was short and stocky, full of life. His hair was short and sandy-colored.

Johnjoe said "I'm John Kavanagh. I was taught by the brothers in Dingle, and I'm a good friend of Brother Leonard."

"A good man, off serving our exiles in Newfoundland," Brother John said.

"I would like to volunteer to help you, but I need a place to sleep," Johnjoe said.

"That we can give you, John. We've converted our classrooms into dormitories, and we would be glad for the help," Brother John said.

"Brother, two weeks from today I'll come with a load of cornmeal and rice from Dublin," said Bewley. "You use your resources well."

"That would be a blessing to us," Brother John replied.

Johnjoe threw himself into the work, helping the brothers clean the tables and get them ready for the following day.

The next day after Johnjoe explained he had learned from the Quakers at their soup kitchen how to boil the stirabout, Brother John had Johnjoe boil the cornmeal in a big steamer. At three o'clock Brother Clement rang a bell attached to the well outside, and dozens of children appeared. The first sitting provided places for half the boys and girls, the other half lining up in the hallway. Brother John said Grace Before Meals, and then he, Johnjoe, and Brother Clement went from table to table with battered silver tureens doling corn porridge into each child's bowl.

"John, keep an eye out for the little ones. Sometimes the bigger lads crowd them out. We have a bit of buttermilk, which we'll give to those who look worse off. That I'll do because the children still have some respect for the habit and collar," said Brother John.

After forty-five minutes, the brothers and Johnjoe had fed 200 children. With something in their stomachs, they grew livelier, not just starving children.

"John, please go out and supervise the games in the courtyard while Brother Clement and I make a start on the wash up. Five footballs are in the shed. Here's the key. Try to keep the boys from maiming each another, not always easy."

"Yes, Brother. These kids could use a bit of fun."

Johnjoe got five games going, three with the bigger boys and two with the smaller. He didn't know what to do with the girls, but they were content to make up their own games in a corner of the courtyard. The children were distracted from their hunger if only for a few hours. They played until it was almost dark.

Johnjoe came in to help the two brothers finish cleaning the tables, leaving them gleaming for the next day.

"You've done great, John," said Brother John. "Take a bit of a rest now, and later you can help Brother Clement and me put the children to bed."

"Fine, Brother. I was wondering if we could cut the hair of these children. We could soap and disinfect them from head lice."

"A grand idea entirely, John. You're a Brothers' boy right enough. I'll get some good soap. We could start with the dormitory boys tomorrow. I'll see if one of the Sisters of Mercy would do the girls. Have you ever seen anyone with the fever on them?"

"Yes, Brother. Me Ma and Da died of it."

"Good God, John, I'm sorry."

"If we can save these little ones here, I would be glad for it."

"You've got a big heart, John."

For Johnjoe, each day merged with the next—preparing the corn porridge, feeding the children, and then supervising them at play. He enjoyed being busy and working through his penance.

Johnjoe and Brother Clement became the house barbers, cutting the hair of the boys in the courtyard just outside the kitchen door. Brother Clement borrowed Mother Evangeline from the Sisters of Mercy convent to cut the hair of the girls, far more sensitive to the loss of their hair than the boys. Brother Clement, Johnjoe, and the Mercy nun used the well water to lather and rinse each child's scalp. In four days the three adults cut the hair, and washed the heads of all 200 children, the only fuss arising from children who had gotten soap in their eyes.

Sleeping in the dormitory, Johnjoe experienced several recurring nightmares, the worst his Ma and Da almost naked, hoisted above the blue waters of the St. Lawrence and dumped into a rowboat to be carried to the shore. Johnjoe stood frozen near the body cart. He began to rush towards his parents, but Father Moylan held him back. Johnjoe cried out, "Ma" and "Da" in his sleep when Brother John rushed into the dormitory to see what was wrong. Johnjoe woke up, looked around him, and realized he was in his cot. "A nightmare, Brother. Bad memories. I'm sorry I bothered you."

"Not at all. I have them myself, especially when the little ones catch the fever. Thank God we can call on Dr. Desmond for help."

Many nights Johnjoe slept easily, tired from chasing the little ones all day. Sometimes he dreamt of the Mullins girls as they watched their father slip away. He wanted to marry Mary Mullins. Tall, with a freckled face and ebony hair, she was growing into loveliness. While he was away, some farmer's son could snatch her up. Even Tommy Linnane said she was pretty. And here he was still running from Packenham. He wondered if he would he ever have a life of his own.

* * *

The painting from the late nineteenth century (*Evicted* by Lady Butler, 1890, University College, Dublin) shows how Irish art had changed since the Famine years. *Evicted* constitutes a new direction in Irish rural art. Portraying the after-effects of the destruction of the peasant woman's cabin, the beauty of the landscape (the Wicklow hills) complements the plight of the inhabitants. 'She too is a victim of historic exploitation, with no rights over the land she inhabits.'

After crushing the aborted rebellion of '48 at Ballingarry, Packenham and his troops returned to their work of tumbling houses, but they had already completed most of the destruction,

137

the countryside littered with broken-down cottages. After Major Mahon's death, his estate lay vacant for a while. With the murder of five more landlords in the west of Ireland, the family couldn't sell the estate because Englishmen were afraid to become landlords and thus targets for killing. Finally, the major's son-in-law, Sullivan-Mahon, who had adopted his father-in-law's last name, came from England to take over the holdings, one of his first orders of business to hector the local dragoons about the murder of Major Mahon. He sent a messenger to Dingle demanding Captain Packenham visit him at his estate. When the captain rode up, he found everything in good trim, the house newly painted and the grounds manicured.

The new owner opened the door to the captain's knock, and though at first discomfited by the black eye patch, didn't offer the guest the customary courtesy of tea. Sullivan-Mahon brought the captain into a bright dining room furnished with Queen Anne sideboards, table, and chairs. During their interview Sullivan-Mahon purposely kept the captain standing while he himself sat at the head of the table. Drawing a scowl from his host, the captain grabbed a chair and thrust himself into it.

"Captain, find the murderer of my father-in-law."

"We've tried, Sir, tracking our suspect as far as Listowel, but we were told the young man has sailed to St. John's, Newfoundland."

"One of our colonies. Write the dragoons there to apprehend the man— which you should have already done. And do it immediately before I take the matter up with your superiors. Then report back to me."

As Captain Packenham rode back to Dingle, he passed the spot near the Garfinney Bridge where the major had been shot. He thought to himself it's no wonder these landlords are killed, the way they treat people, unaware of the irony of his thinking.

After his interrogation by Sullivan-Mahon, Captain Packenham simmered in his barracks. He wrote to Captain Whittingham, the leader of the dragoons in St. John's, Newfoundland, and asked him to question roundly Brother Leonard and to see if Kevane was hiding there. Whittingham wrote back that Brother Leonard and his colleagues had established an orphanage, Mt. Cashel, for those children whose parents had died of Famine-related diseases. Questioned about Johnjoe, Brother Leonard answered that he had last seen him in Listowel, which was true. Brother Leonard did not volunteer that a letter from Father Cavanagh had informed him that Johnjoe would be going off with the Quakers to Skibbereen.

Whittingham's letter infuriated Packenham—lied to again by the priest Cavanagh that the boy was in St. John's. More than ever, he was convinced of Kevane's guilt. And to think he had allowed the bastard to slip through his fingers hours after the murder.

Packenham decided on a new tack. He would try to outguess his adversary. No reports of him leaving the country for America or anywhere else had surfaced. He wondered where the villain would go. The most dangerous place in the country was Skibbereen, West Cork, where the fever raged.

The one connection Packenham could make with Johnjoe's escape was the clergy: here in Dingle, Tralee, and Listowel. If Kevane was in Skibbereen doing God knows what, he would have to find a place to stay, maybe with these Christian Brothers. Packenham discussed his theory with Lieutenant Thomas and asked him to question the brothers in Dingle to find out if they had a school also in Skibbereen.

Looking more careworn than even a few weeks before, Brother Gerald opened the door to Thomas: "Good morning, Lieutenant."

"Brother, I'm wondering if your order maintains a school or a monastery in Skibbereen or Cork."

"Yes, St. Nessan's School on Sullivan's Quay in Cork City. I taught there myself some years ago. The school like this one now serves meals instead of teaching students. Skibbereen is some miles west of the school where Brother John serves one meal a day to 200 children. It's the worst place for disease in the country. Trevelyan refused to send aid there."

"Thanks, Brother."

"Lieutenant, you seem a good and decent man. Fever and death stalk the streets there. Be careful."

When Thomas reported to Packenham, the captain was adamant: "Fever or no, we're going there."

"Sir, the men won't want to go."

"Lieutenant, the men will go."

Despite much grumbling among them, the dragoons set off early the next morning. After a ride of several hours, they came to the town of Kenmare, badly afflicted with Famine and disease, one of every seven of the population living in the workhouse. They came upon a dead woman laying across the road, a little girl of one or two sucking her lifeless breast. No one had come to remove the child and take the body away for fear of the fever.

Lieutenant Thomas said to Packenham, "We must stop and have the body removed and find care for the child."

"No, Lieutenant. The Bible says 'Let the dead bury the dead.'"

Thomas drew closer to Packenham and said out of earshot of the rest of the troop, "Goddamn you, Patrick. The psalmist says, 'For he delivers the needy when they call, the poor and those who have no helper. He has pity on the weak and the needy, and saves the lives of the needy'. I've never disobeyed you. But this is simple humanity. You can proceed without me or take your gun out and shoot me, but I'm doing this."

Taken aback by his lieutenant, who had never before opposed him, Packenham said, "Well, be quick about it."

Unafraid of catching the fever, Thomas picked up the almost naked baby and brought her to the rectory where he spoke to the pastor, Father Killelea. "Father, this baby's mother is lying dead in the road. Here's five pounds to bury the mother and see to the child."

The priest thanked Thomas.

* * *

One rainy morning Brother John, Brother Clement, and Johnjoe had a few minutes to themselves in the kitchen over tea. "Johnjoe, I'm sure the brothers in Dingle told you of Edmund Rice, our founder. He died in 1844, the year before the Famine."

"Yes, Brother. I remember the Duke of Wellington had told Edmund that all his schools would be closed because of the Penal Laws forbidding an education to Catholics. But he persevered, and Daniel O'Connell succeeded in repealing the Penal Laws."

"Yes," Brother Leonard said, "we still miss Edmund's guidance. Until the Famine abates, we live from day to day. We now feed the boys we once taught. What the future holds is a mystery."

"The Mercy sisters have been a Godsend," said Brother Clement, "especially in Dublin where they go out into the slums to feed and teach poor girls. Here in Cork they also maintain a soup kitchen, and they were the first to receive potatoes from the land surrounding the Mathew Tower built in memory of the temperance priest Mathew Theobald."

"A Mercy nun works in Listowel," Johnjoe said, "Sister Clare, who's kindness itself cooking the stirabout and teaching the girls sewing at St. Michael's."

Brother John smiled as he said, "This is the first time the three of us have had a minute to talk like this. Tell us a bit of yourself, John, if we aren't being too inquisitive."

"Brother, it's a sad tale. My Ma, Da, and I were evicted from our cottage in Ballyristeen outside Dingle and sailed aboard a coffin ship to Canada. My parents died there of fever, thrown into a mass grave, and I made my way back here. I've written a diary of the voyage, and Mr. Bewley told me the Quakers would publish it if it's worthy."

Shocked by his story, the two brothers sat silently. "Your story is heartrending, John," said Brother Clement. "What a good man you are to have gone through all that."

"Yes, Brother, but I always had people to help me—Mr. Whyte, a journalist aboard ship, Father Moylan at Grosse Ile, Canon Long and Brother Leonard in Dingle, Father Cavanagh in Listowel, and the Quakers."

"Don't you wonder what it all means," said Brother John, "Edmund Rice's trials, the suffering of you and your family, the calamity our poor country is enduring."

"Father Moylan told me that God didn't cause all this pain, that men are responsible," Johnjoe said. "We've built up a powerful hatred of England, the source of much of our misery."

"You're right, Johnjoe," Brother Clement said. "Our rebellion was a farce, but the English hold it against us so—as if we should just lie down and die."

Johnjoe and Brother John were working in the kitchen the next day boiling and stirring the cornmeal when Johnjoe sensed that the brother was badly depressed. "Brother, you seem upset."

"I should be glad because a local farmer, Mick Dennehy, came in and gave us his cow which we can use for meat and bones for our soup. But he told me a story I can't get out of my mind. A couple was traveling from Anaglen when the wife asked the husband for a bit of bread. This happened three times, and the husband was filled with the hunger."

"Finally the man said to himself, 'If this goes on any more, I'll starve'. Enraged, he threw his wife in the lake and drowned her. Coming to his senses, the husband was remorseful for what he had done and drowned himself. When the bodies were recovered, it was found the mother was carrying three little ones with her. Since then the lake bears the name of 'The Lake of the Five People.'"

Johnjoe took over stirring the cornmeal, the steam making his face flush while Brother John sat at the table for his tea. "Sure, I can see why you're depressed, Brother. Two days in Skibbereen were enough for me. Coffins stacked against the side of cottages and then in the graveyard bodies thrown in pits with no coffins at all. I don't know how Vicar Townsend keeps his head at all."

"I heard he just died of the fever, John."

"God, I'm sorry. He was a good man, Brother. Mr. Bewley and I were with him just before we came here."

When Johnjoe had finished at the boiler, he sat down across from Brother John for tea. Brother John said, "Mick Dennehy did tell me a hopeful tale. He was out in his field, which has a fine spring well when he saw a mother dragging her stout little girl to the well and the child roaring. The mother was about to drown the girl. He ran over to the woman and asked, 'What in the devil's name are you doing?'"

"Oh Sir," she said, "this one is eating me out of house and home, starving these two little ones" whom she was dragging with her other hand. "It's better for God to take her and save these."

"Woman, don't murder your child. Come to our cottage and have a bite to eat."

"Dennehy told the story to his wife who fed the mother and children potatoes and buttermilk. After they had eaten and taken a rest, the woman and her three children left, the mother promising never again to think of doing away with her child."

Johnjoe finished cleaning the kitchen as the cornmeal simmered, ready for the afternoon feeding.

The next day while serving the children their porridge, Johnjoe noticed that Kevin Kearns, a lively six-year-old, had purple bruises over his face and an angry gash near his left ear.

"Kevin," Johnjoe said, "you were fighting."

"No, Sir," the boy replied. "Farmer Barry beat me for stealing grains of oats from his field. I had a little bag that I was bringing home to my mother to cook dinner."

"Barry's farm is near," said Johnjoe.

"About two miles from town on the road to Ballydehob, Sir."

That afternoon Johnjoe asked Brother Clement to supervise the boys at their games for him because he had an errand.

Johnjoe walked to Barry's farm, a neat, whitewashed cottage

with a vegetable garden outside it and well-tended fields. On his way Johnjoe passed several destroyed cottages. The farmer's wife told him that Barry was out in the fields cutting hay and rye. When Johnjoe approached Barry, a hulking man with a red face and a cap on, the farmer said, "You're a stranger."

"John Kavanagh from St. Nessan's School. You gave a thrashing to a little boy for stealing grain."

The man blushed and said, "The thieving little bastard would have me robbed blind. He was lucky he didn't fall into one of my man-traps and drown."

"It didn't matter that he was trying to feed his family," Johnjoe said.

"Sure I can't feed the countryside," Barry said.

"You're surrounded by tumbled cottages. It doesn't bother you to sell food to England while your neighbors starve and die."

Turning red, Barry said, "You have no right to judge me. If some of those louts had been better farmers, they would be still alive."

"There are starving children dying in the road."

"I pay my taxes to support the workhouse."

"What was the value of the oats the boy was trying to take?" Johnjoe asked.

"A few shillings, I suppose," Barry said.

Reaching into his pocket, Johnjoe grabbed five shillings and flung them at Barry, jabbing his finger into the bigger man's chest. "Here's for the oats. If you ever lay a hand on that boy again, it's more than five shillings you'll be getting. I'll be back in a few days to see that you destroy those mantraps." Johnjoe turned and walked away.

* * *

During Johnjoe's absence from St. Nessan's that afternoon, Packenham and his dragoons had arrived at the school. Packenham didn't bother with the formality of knocking on the door. He walked right through the hallway to the kitchen where he met Brother John cleaning the cooking vat.

"I'm hunting for a murderer, Johnjoe Kevane," Packenham said.

"No one here by that name," Brother John replied.

"We'll see," said Packenham, sending his dragoons scurrying in all directions and scattering the children playing games outside. One bold boy, Kevin Reilly, knocked aside by Packenham, kicked a football that landed high on the captain's back. Whirling about, Packenham looked for the offender who had the sense to disappear into a crowd of his mates.

Brother Clement grabbed the boy and warned him, "You eejit trying to get yourself killed. Get into the shed and hide yourself until these dragoons are gone."

After a search of the school and the outbuildings, the dragoons found no sign of Johnjoe. On their way out, Packenham told Brother John, "We'll be back, mind. And if we find you're concealing a murderer, I'll tear this place down."

When he had returned to the school, Brother John met Johnjoe at the door: "The dragoons are just after leaving. They were looking for Johnjoe Kevane."

Turning ashen, Johnjoe said, "Yes, Brother, they're hunting me. If I'm a danger to you, I'll leave now."

"I've a better idea. Should Mr. Bewley arrive tomorrow as he said, he could smuggle you out among his corn and rice sacks. I know that you're a good man, no matter what the dragoons say. We've just got to keep a sharp eye out for tonight until we can get you clear."

"Brother, a favor. A farmer named Barry beat Kevin Kearns for stealing a few grains of oats. I paid Barry five shillings and warned him never to touch the boy again. I also warned him to destroy some mantraps in his field. Please keep an eye on the boy for me."

"Yes, John."

As he had promised, Bewley arrived at St. Nessan's the following morning with a load of cornmeal and rice. Johnjoe spoke to him, "Mr. Bewley, I need your help. The dragoons are hunting me, I'm hoping you would hide me away in the corn and rice sacks on your wagon."

"Gladly, Johnjoe. I trust you and have reason to be wary of dragoon justice."

Johnjoe thanked Brother John and Brother Clement who were sorry to see him go. They pressed upon him a few shillings for his journey. Bewley and Brother John helped hide him under some canvas among the corn and rice sacks, some of which were empty and some that were to be dropped off at Ballydehob.

Johnjoe hated running away again from Packenham who was like a dog gnawing on a bone. He wouldn't let go. As they left Cork, it was raining hard, too foul for the dragoons to be on the road. However, as they drove three miles from the city, six drenched dragoons rode toward them. Packenham stopped Bewley. "This is terrible weather for you to be out."

Even with the rain, Johnjoe could make out every word. If the dragoons pulled off the tarp, he was poised to jump from the wagon and make a run for it, but he wouldn't get far because the soldiers were on horseback.

"I'm Joseph Bewley carrying a load of corn and rice to the poor souls in Ballydehob, Captain, where I'm to pick up a friend, Mr. Todhunter."

"I'm chasing a murderer, Kevane. I'll hang him," Packenham said.

"You sound very sure of yourself, Captain."

"I am. Were it not for those lying Catholic clergy, his neck would have been stretched already."

"Captain, violence breeds only more violence."

"I'm not paid to discuss Quaker pacifist views, Bewley. Be on your way."

Many miles further on, the downpour became so bad that the road was muck, and Bewley stopped his horse and cart near a scalpin, which gave some shelter from the storm. A piece of canvas and dense shrubbery kept off some of the rain. Johnjoe said, "Mr. Bewley, Packenham has been after me for months now. He tore down our cottage two years ago."

"Johnjoe, my heart tells me you're a good man. I'll do all I can to protect you. My plan is to pick up Mr. Todhunter in Ballydehob. He's in charge of our fisheries' program, and the three of us will journey north to the Claddagh in Galway where we need workers. Father Cavanagh told me you have experience on the sea."

"Yes, I've sailed to Canada and back and fished in Dingle Bay," said Johnjoe. "So I know my way around a ship."

"And you have the Irish, so that will be a help to us because that's the only language used by the fishermen there. We hope that they'll allow us to show them modern methods of fishing."

A horse was tied to a bush near the ditch, and they found a priest, Hugh Quigley, taking shelter in the same scalp. He was a curate, a pastor's assistant, in Ballydehob. The three introduced themselves when Johnjoe asked the priest what his work was like in this terrible place. The priest was anxious to talk: "We rise at four o'clock when not obliged to attend a night call, and to proceed a distance from four to seven miles to hold stations of Confession for the convenience of the poor country people, who flock in thousands to prepare themselves for the death they look to as inevitable."

"Father, these are the worst of times for all of us. Vicar Townsend of Skibbereen has died of the fever," Bewley said.

"I knew him," said Father Quigley, "a good shepherd to his people. No man could have done more."

* * *

Back at St. Michael's in Listowel, Mary Mullins had once more to draw on her own resources with Johnjoe gone. Under Sister Clare's tutelage, Mary had become the most accomplished knitter and seamstress of all the girls. She told Nellie and Josie, "Sure, I'm your mother now, and I'll never leave you. It's important that you become good seamstresses, so we can earn our keep. We'll stay together—no orphanage in Dublin or trip to America or Australia for us."

Josie and Nellie cried, grateful that their future was settled. Even without Johnjoe, they had Mary.

Chapter 18

After their fruitless search for Kevane in Skibbereen and Cork, the dragoons returned to Dingle. Packenham's headaches were getting worse, and now he had a new one: Queen Victoria would be making a visit to Ireland. The captain knew all the dragoons in the country would be called from their duties to safeguard her. He wouldn't be able to hunt Kevane for the duration of her stay.

*　*　*

Tommy Linnane still smarted from his whipping by Mr. Gray, but instead of deterring him, the humiliation whetted his appetite for revenge against Johnjoe. He had sneaked around St. Michael's for weeks, begging meals from Sister Clare. Tommy never believed that his nemesis had fled to Newfoundland, deserting his precious Mullins sisters. Sister Clare had warned the girls not to talk with him, making Tommy all the more suspicious that information was to be had of Johnjoe's whereabouts. Father Cavanagh was a threat because the priest rousted him from St. Michael's every time he saw him—though the old man had saved him from a further whipping from Mr. Gray. To console the Mullins girls, the priest told them of Johnjoe's trip to the Claddagh, only a few hours away, to work with the Quakers. Tommy thought perhaps he could get his two sisters, Maureen and Eileen, to wheedle information out of Josie or Nellie, the two youngest Mullins girls. Mary, the eldest, would see through him right away.

One October day after receiving a few coins for breaking stones at the workhouse, Tommy scurried into town to buy candies for his sisters, who would dearly love them. Using the sweets as a pretext for visiting them, he sneaked by Sister Clare working in the kitchen and made straight for the girls' dormitory where his sisters were working on the knitting the nun had assigned them.

"Girls, I've brought you some treats." This was all too rare in a starving country. The sisters were thrilled. "I want to know where Johnjoe is."

"It doesn't matter where Johnjoe has gone," Maureen, the elder of the two sisters said.

"Never mind, Maureen. It's important to me," replied Tommy. "I'll bring you more candy if you can find out where Johnjoe is off to," Tommy said.

But the conversation got no further when Sister Clare glided into the room. "I suppose you're up to devilment, Tommy."

"I've brought treats for my sisters."

But Sister Clare was not fooled for a minute. "Well, you've given them, so be gone with you."

He couldn't argue with Sister Clare, but Tommy had planted the seed with his sisters. With information about Johnjoe, he felt sure he could approach Mr. Gray again, but he must be certain of his facts. One thrashing was enough.

* * *

After dropping off one load of corn and rice at Ballydehob in West Cork, Bewley and Johnjoe met Mr. Todhunter, famous even among The Society of Friends for his devotion to Famine relief. Todhunter had aided the Irish fishing industry by having the British admiralty chart the bottom of the ocean up to twenty miles out to sea around the coasts, a task never done before.

The three travelers resumed their journey and passed through the village of Mallow, once a busy agricultural town in the Blackwater Valley. Hanging from an iron balcony in front of the jailhouse were twin gallows, their trapdoors yawning emptily below as a warning to thieves. Unlike England where the authorities erected wooden gallows only for hangings, Irish jails used them as permanent fixtures. Johnjoe shuddered as he thought of his own neck in the noose should Packenham get his hands on him.

As they rode further north, they came against a sheriff armed with a musket while riding a horse and leading a man with his hands tied and a rope around his neck. When Bewley asked about the prisoner, the sheriff said, "A sheep stealer, Sir. He'll hang. At least he left the head and the sheep's bell on the mountain above so the shepherd would know the poor creature didn't wander off."

Bewley addressed the prisoner: "You killed the sheep."

"To feed me wife and four little ones," he answered.

The sheriff said, "They roast the sheep away from home because the smell would give them away to the neighbors if they cooked it in their cottage. They hide some in the woods and bring home enough for a meal."

"Sheriff, of what value is the sheep," Bewley said

"It's about ten shillings, Sir."

"Sheriff, I respect your enforcing the law, but the man's family is starving," Bewley said.

"Sir, I can't help that. Sure the countryside is famished entirely."

"Sheriff, let's save a man's life. Here is ten shillings for the animal and three for yourself doing your duty," Bewley said. "Let the man go back and get the sheep to feed his family."

"I don't know, Sir. I have to keep the law."

"This way," Bewley said, "the farmer will be compensated, you'll be freeing yourself of the burden of this man's death, and also feeding his family."

"Since you put it that way, Sir, I'll agree. Thomas Boland, you should get down on your knees to thank these Quakers."

Bewley gave the sheriff thirteen shillings, and the man left for town.

Thomas Boland thanked Bewley who gave him three shillings: "Sir, you've saved my life and my family's. God bless." The man scampered up the mountain to retrieve his meat.

"What a country we live in," Todhunter said, "where a man can't feed his family."

On their way to Galway, the bay gleaming just west and north of them and the wide ocean beyond it, the three travelers met a lone woman, Asenath Nicholson, the lady whom Bewley had told Johnjoe of earlier, riding in a coach driven by a pock-faced man with a cap pulled tight on his head. "Mrs. Nicholson," Bewley said, "I shouldn't be surprised to see you turn up anywhere in Ireland."

After introductions, Mrs. Nicholson said, "In these mountainous areas, as beautiful as they are, the poor people are burying bodies between two boards with a straw rope around them. It's almost too much to bear."

"Yes," Bewley replied, "but we've seen worse in Skibbereen."

"In these places the poor are kind, leaving the cabin door open and a fire lit to welcome the stranger," she said. "Many is the time the people get up and give me their one bed, the fire having been kept bright throughout the night."

Johnjoe asked her where she was traveling. "To Dublin and then home to America," Mrs. Nicholson said. "The poverty and suffering have so exhausted me I can't stand it any more."

Johnjoe answered, "We wish you well. Thanks for what you've done for our people."

"Amen to that, Mrs. Nicholson," Bewley said. "I'm about at the end of my own tether."

With those blessings she parted from them.

* * *

Mary Mullins was angry. "Sure not a word from Johnjoe for months," she complained to Sister Clare. "He said he loves me, the eejit. I've half a mind to have Father Cavanagh arrange a marriage for me to some farmer."

"Go ahead," Sister Clare said. "But you'll not find a better man than Johnjoe Kevane in a long day's march."

"Sure, you're always defending him. Saint Johnjoe."

"Look here to me, Mary. Johnjoe has suffered things that you know nothing about. He had no choice but to leave. If he hasn't written you or visited here, he has a reason."

"Sure, he's your favorite, Sister. Johnjoe Perfect. In your eyes he can do no wrong, but he left us here to fend for ourselves."

"He couldn't drag you and the girls with him—with no money or place to stay."

"He's probably hunting for some new colleen."

"Enough, Mary. You'll have me crazy. Get out of my kitchen."

* * *

On their journey to Galway, Todhunter, Bewley, and Johnjoe stopped at the Cliffs of Moher, five miles of black outcropping up to 700 feet high, assaulted by the Atlantic and plunging straight down into it with no scree at the bottom—a combination of vertical drop with serpentine undulations hypnotic to the eye. Stripes of layers of shale and sand gave the cliffs a rough surface. The three travelers marveled as they looked down upon the vast gray Atlantic yawning below. From there the travelers journeyed fifteen miles to "The Burren," or "stony place," 300 square kilometers of limestone, bordered on the west by Galway Bay.

Johnjoe explained to the two Quakers that he had changed his name to John Kavanagh, the anglicised version of his Irish name. Talking of fishing, Johnjoe explained that for his family herring was a luxury to be eaten with potatoes. Johnjoe and his father would set out in a two-man curragh and fish in Dingle Bay, just a mile from their cottage. Using seines with lead weights and floaters on the surface, the two would trap the fish inside the net by pulling a rope on top that tied the ends of the net together. But even in Dingle Bay surrounded by mountains and much calmer than the ocean east and south of them, the Kevanes were wary of sudden gales that could overturn their curragh and drown them. "The whole time we were out," explained Johnjoe, "me Ma would wait for us on the shore, the rosary beads twisting in her fingers that we'd be safe. In the bow of the boat, she always kept a container of holy water blessed by the priest. Da and I would chuckle at her fears, but she paid us no mind."

"You're a swimmer then," said Todhunter.

"Yes. Me Da made me learn to be a strong swimmer. He taught me how to look for riptides where two currents meet and change the color of the water by churning up the sand below. If you're caught in one, you have to tread water, and then swim at an angle to the shore."

"You always caught herring, lad," said Todhunter.

"Yes, and the odd salmon. On our voyage to Canada, we caught a whole bunch of cod off Newfoundland, the best fish I ever tasted," Johnjoe said.

"You went to Canada and back, Mr. Bewley told me, Johnjoe. I can't believe you made it."

"It was the worst time of my life when me Ma and Da died of the fever at Grosse Ile. All I had was home," Johnjoe said. "I was determined to make my way back. The captain of the *Jeanie Johnston*, a timber ship, hired me on. We landed in Tralee."

The two Quakers became silent and didn't press the boy for any details, all too fresh in his mind.

As they rode into Galway, the travelers saw a section in the southwest part of the town nearest the ocean called the "Claddagh," Irish for "stony beach," with jagged rows of beehive huts of dry stone covered with thatched roofs built next to one another, no roads leading to them, the settlements called "clochans."

Todhunter said, "These are a suspicious people, Johnjoe, and we'll have our work cut out for us. Thank God you speak Irish, which is all they use here. We'll have to tread softly to befriend them. We're to meet a Father Rushe, a Dominican priest, who founded a piscatorial school, where they train children in advanced methods of fishing. They've also set up a soup kitchen at the school. The Claddagh king and his men trust him, so he's important to our efforts."

Todunter had explained to Johnjoe that a year before the Quakers had sent Joseph Crosfield and William Forster to survey and report on conditions in the Claddagh. They learned that many of the Claddagh fishermen had pawned their nets and tackle to buy food.

Todhunter had known all this when he went to the Claddagh. As guests of the village, Todhunter and Johnjoe shared a cottage with the son of the King or Admiral, the head fisherman.

Todhunter explained to Johnjoe that the boats the Claddagh men used, hookers and curraghs, had serious drawbacks. Often Claddagh fishermen rowed twenty-five miles to the fishing grounds in the Atlantic and feared sudden squalls when returning to shore.

The men of the Claddagh elected their own king or admiral, a well-respected fisherman who did not stand out from others, except for the white sails of his hooker contrasting with the red brown sails of the rest of the fleet. The admiral's job was to settle any internal disputes, the village so tightly knit that outside intervention was unheard of.

With Johnjoe as translator for the Irish-speaking admiral, Todhunter was to meet with him to discuss how the Quakers could help the Claddagh fishermen. The Quakers had studied the Irish fisheries and determined that a trawler could serve as a floating base for the hookers and curraghs, especially in bad weather when the fishermen were far from shore.

Johnjoe learned that at the piscatorial school in town, the priests and nuns instructed all Claddagh children in how to read and write, trained the girls in lace making and net mending, and taught the boys sound fishing practices.

Joseph Bewley departed to the model farm at Colmanstown, while Todhunter and Johnjoe stayed on at the Claddagh with Donald Doherty, the admiral's son. Donald loved telling Johnjoe stories of the "sunfish" or giant basking shark, second only to the whale shark in size for its species.

Because the community was so insular, people marrying only other Claddagh members, the village assigned names to distinguish among those with the same surnames. The custom was to give names associated with fish, for example, Michael the Mackerel and Peter the Pike.

Todhunter, Father Rushe, and Johnjoe went to meet Admiral Doherty. Like all the other Claddagh homes, the admiral's cottage sparkled. Walls were two or three feet thick built of mortared stone up to a height of eight feet carrying beams on which thatch lay. A wooden ladder ascended to a loft where the admiral's daughter Siobhan slept. Several layers of whitewash kept the draught out. The floor consisted of hard-packed earth. On one wall hung a wooden crucifix, on another a picture of Mary, Our Lady of Galway. A black kettle hung on an iron hook over a burning fire of peat. Fishing tackle, nets, and oilskins hung on the walls. Above the hearth burned a candle before a picture of the Sacred Heart.

Mrs. Doherty served the guests tea and then scurried out. The admiral introduced his wife's mother, Granny Lydon, who sat by the fire knitting, giving the guests a glimmer of a smile. The people of the Claddagh respected grandmothers as teachers of children, especially with the men out at sea and their wives selling fish at the market.

Admiral Doherty was in his thirties, with hair of iron and black and skin weathered red by sun and wind. With Johnjoe serving as translator, the men sat around a wooden kitchen table in straight timber chairs. Todhunter explained that his mission was to help the men of the Claddagh improve their fishing. Because the Quakers didn't hold with titles, Todhunter addressed the admiral as "Mister."

Todhunter followed the advice of Father Rushe and loaned the admiral money for the fishermen to retrieve their nets and tackle from pawn. Everything was going well until Todhunter said, "We would like to provide you the use of a trawler for fishing in the bay and further out in the ocean." The admiral glowered at Todhunter. "We'll have no trawler in our bay." The Claddagh fishermen believed that a trawler disturbed the ocean floor and reduced the stock of fish. Todhunter took no offense, saying, "We will do nothing you are opposed to," and the meeting ended cordially, the admiral already pleased that more of his men would be back on the sea, their nets redeemed from pawn.

In truth the admiral was worried. While the Claddagh had escaped typhus, which ravaged the rest of Ireland, cholera and dysentery struck his village, and many families had emigrated to America or Canada, pawning their heirloom Claddagh rings of gold to pay for the journey. Still others had joined the British navy.

On their way back to their cottage, Todhunter told Johnjoe and Father Rushe, "We will do as we said and advance loans to as many fishermen as need them to remove their boats, nets, and tackle from pawn. We could simply give them the money, but the men must keep their dignity. Father, it would help us if you could bring Mr. Doherty around to our way of thinking about the loan of a trawler—if only on a trial basis of three months. If the trawler doesn't improve fishing, the men will at least have their hookers and curraghs back."

"That's a fair offer, Mr. Todhunter. I'll do what I can," said Father Rushe.

The next day Todhunter brought additional money to the admiral, and soon more hookers were sailing.

The townspeople were thrilled because the men of Claddagh were back at sea. Years before they had passed a law forbidding the fishermen to have gardens because they were always to be fishing. As partial compensation for this restriction, Claddagh wives were always given first place in line at market.

During the summer, the fishermen saved herring and mackerel for the winter, and cured them in barrels of salt and water before hanging them to dry and smoke.

Todhunter explained that despite their industriousness and courage, the men of the Claddagh practiced outmoded fishing practices. They watched diving birds as signs of herring and banged stones on the side of their boats to turn the fish into their nets. Todhunter explained to Johnjoe and Father Rushe. "The Dutch do much better with the herring using drift nets and then gutting the fish right on deck and salting them for preservation. The Scots do the same, even putting the gutted and salted herrings in barrels to shrink and cure right on deck. When a squall is approaching, the ships bring the herring right to shore where groups of three women, two gutterers and a packer salt the cleaned fish and place them in barrels. The gutterers have to wrap their fingers in bandages to prevent cutting themselves with the sharp knives."

Father Rushe listened and said, "These are good ideas, Mr. Todhunter. You've done your research well, and God bless you for it."

Todhunter said, "The admiral still doesn't trust us."

"Yes," Johnjoe answered, "but a sense of desperation hangs over the village and may convince them to give you a fair hearing."

"I agree. Mr. Todhunter, please don't lose your patience with them. They're like the Jews in the Bible—'a proud and stiff-necked people.'"

*　*　*

By midsummer all the Claddagh hookers were back at sea. On August 15th, the Feast of the Assumption of the Blessed Virgin Mary into heaven, the Claddagh held its annual blessing of the bay and of the hookers, the time coinciding with the herring run. The day was mild with only a slight wind from the southwest. Todhunter, Johnjoe, and Donald had their own hooker, directed by Sammy the

Salmon, its three brown sails ruffling in the wind. The water was slate-gray with a blue sky above. As the head priest, Father Rushe stood near the mast of the lead hooker wearing church vestments. From alongside came the admiral's hooker festooned with white silk for the occasion. 200 boats began to circle around the two lead boats when the admiral doffed his white hat to signal all was ready for the service. Father Rushe prayed for a time and then blessed the bay three times, after which all the men knelt in their boats and recited the rosary. To conclude the ceremony, all the boats took a turn around Galway Bay before returning to shore.

"I'm not of your religion, Johnjoe, but that was a holy and impressive ceremony," said Mr. Todhunter.

"Yes," said Johnjoe, "I hope God will answer our prayers."

* * *

Donald Doherty asked Johnjoe if he would like to accompany him on his rounds of work and then fish for cod. Johnjoe agreed. First they collected baitfish and mussels from the shore in buckets and then walked to the base of the cliffs at the edge of the bay where the women had put lobsters into holes in the rocks at half tide. The two then fed the baitfish to a dozen fat lobsters, which would grow even bigger. When they were full-sized, they would be taken out and eaten or sold at market.

When they were finished, Donald went to his father, the admiral, and asked permission to take a hooker to go fishing. The admiral said, "Yes, but mind you stay within the bay for fear of a squall." Only the three Aran Islands thirty miles west stood between Galway Bay and the open sea, America the next large land mass.

Donald got them some line and hooks while Johnjoe collected more baitfish. Donald and Johnjoe pulled a small hooker marked with the sign of the Claddagh on its sail, a heart held by two hands with a crown above, symbolizing love, friendship and loyalty. Donald showed Johnjoe how to work the mainsail and the two foresails. The two hugged their boat to the cliffs near the shore, knowing that the Admiral and the other fishermen would be monitoring them. Their lines well baited, Donald and Johnjoe caught a dozen cod and ling, the larger member of the cod family. As they turned for home, a huge swell hit them broadside, driving Johnjoe into the water. Donald righted the boat and extended an oar to Johnjoe who clambered back inside the boat.

"God, it's cold," Johnjoe said. "And it's summer."

Despite their spill, the young men had preserved their catch, which they brought to the admiral. "Well done," he said. "But by the looks of you, John, you've had a taste of saltwater." He gave the fish to his wife for the market, but handed two big cod to Johnjoe and Donald: "For your dinner. You've earned it."

* * *

One calm night Paul the Porpoise received permission from the admiral to fish. From the southwest a storm exploded and drove their light curragh across the water. The men attempted to use their nets as an anchor, but the hurricane wind shot their curragh south. The fierce spray lashed them for seven hours, ripping their clothes from their bodies. Donald woke Johnjoe, and they went to look for the men. At three in the morning a huge wave hurled the fishermen onto the shore where a search party rescued them. Johnjoe and Donald threw blankets around the men and dragged them back to the village, their hands swollen from rowing, their eyes blinded by salt from the sea.

* * *

On most days Johnjoe accompanied Donald to the piscatorial school where the priests taught them how to take soundings of the ocean floor. Because huge outcroppings of rocks lay on the bottom of the sea, nets could be torn easily or lost entirely. It was important to know what lay beneath the water. The priests taught them that the lighter English nets were not strong enough for the rougher Irish seas.

*　*　*

One evening Johnjoe attended an "American wake," the Irish name for a party held for an emigrant about to leave for the United States. William Bolton had saved his money for a trip to New York, anxious to try his fortune in the new world. A mixture of gaiety and sadness, the wake drew in all the neighbors, including the admiral, sorry to lose a good fisherman and fearful that others might follow his example. The Irish believed in "bringing one another out," the emigrant in New York sending money home to help a sibling come to America. Bolton was single, twenty-two, and had family to care for his aging parents. Years of bad weather and poor fishing had discouraged him. Still, leaving was a heartache, seeing his parents, family, and friends for perhaps the last time before leaving for Cobh, the embarkation point for America the next morning. Johnjoe sat in a corner, listening to the music and the tales. Earlier he had advised Bolton to bring extra provisions for the voyage and a chamber pot, counsel that the young man followed. None in the Claddagh had Johnjoe's experience of crossing the ocean, a fact he kept to himself.

As soon as he felt he had stayed long enough for the sake of courtesy, Johnjoe slipped away.

Chapter 19

One late August morning the Claddagh shark spotter was smoking his pipe high on the cliffs when he raised a cry, and the village women hung red petticoats on ropes strung from gables, the sign to the village that the man had spied a basking shark following a line of spouting porpoises feeding near the surface and going into bays. Donald had told Johnjoe that the second-largest shark is fairly easy to spot, the locals calling it a sunfish because it swam close to the surface. The village erupted. Donald, Johnjoe, Sammy the Salmon, and Paddy the Pike filled one of the hookers and charged off into the surf.

Up in the cliffs, the men attached chains with ropes and a cable and wrapped them around a large black boulder sitting in a cleft with the end tied to a harpoon, which they ran down to the shore to the lead hooker. Nine other hookers shot from the shore armed with chains, knives, and ropes. The hookers flew through the water, the men rowing backwards towards the monster.

Like some avenging warrior of Homer, the spearman stood with his harpoon in the lead boat, the cable and rope trailing him from shore. Because the basking shark swam on the surface at about four miles per hour, the blue-brown behemoth made an easy target, but dangerous too. The giant fish often dragged out to sea a boat that was never seen again. Sammy the Salmon yelled over the shouts of the other men, "This one will light the village for six months."

From the liver of the great fish, the fishermen would harvest 300 gallons of oil to light their lanterns if they could bring it home. The spearman's boat got close to the shark, water leaking from its side. He then thrust the spear deep into the gray stripe beneath its large fin, and the sea exploded, blood and water filling the air. Whirling its ten tons to the sky, the maddened fish leaped and smashed the boat of Johnjoe and his companions into matchsticks; and with a flick of his tail drove the men into the deep. As the great shark thrashed around them, it drove Sammy the Salmon to the bottom of the ocean forever. The shark straightened for a run out to sea, and Donald Doherty hung on to the cable as a lifeline that would carry him only to his death.

Surfacing from the roiling water, Johnjoe swam out to Donald and pried his friend's fingers one by one from the cable, freeing him so that he could get the boy back to the approaching hookers. Because Donald had swallowed a lot of water, Johnjoe held his head above the surface in a body carry until other hookers arrived. The men in the nearest hooker hauled in Donald, Johnjoe, and Paddy the Pike. The fishermen heaved on Donald's chest until he spewed out seawater and vomit, gasping for breath. Just a few yards away in agony over his son, the admiral watched the scene unfold. Once the admiral had beached his boat, he leaped into the foam and ran over to his son. Though bruised and bloodied, the boy had survived his battle with the shark. Tears mingling with the salt spray, the admiral embraced Johnjoe, "'Twas you who saved him. None of the rest of us could have reached him in time." Strangely, the Claddagh fishermen were not good swimmers. It took an outsider to save the admiral's son.

Paddy the Pike had narrowly escaped death, and he knew it. Coming over to Johnjoe, he clapped him on the back and said, "You're a brave lad. When the fish knocked us from the boat, he blotted out the sun."

The drama was not yet over, as the black rock in the cleft with its chains still jumped and danced. After almost an hour, the ropes and

163

cable went taut, and everyone in the village hauled on the cable to pull the monster to shore. Joy was mingled with sorrow in the Claddagh as Sammy the Salmon had given his life to the sea, at rest on the ocean floor. Claddagh families viewed drownings with superstition, often not searching for lost bodies because they believed the sea claimed its own. But Johnjoe had saved Donald, and the black and brown giant lay at their feet. As Johnjoe went to examine the sleek mound of the beast, he thought it a shame to butcher something so beautiful. The village would eat the shark meat for days. He wondered if anyone in the Claddagh shared his feeling. He thought not.

The village held a wake in Sammy the Salmon's cottage that night, old ladies and Sammy's widow mourning, wailing over his death with outbursts and shrieks of lamentation. "Keening" was an Irish tradition at wakes; some old women were professional keeners come to wakes to pray and cry over the dead person. The women would sway to and fro while the lead keener, usually the oldest woman, would utter cries and praise for the deceased. Meanwhile on the other side of the cottage, the men engaged in bantering and drinking as if in opposition to the expressions of grief of the women on the other side of the cottage.

The neighbors brought in extra chairs along with much porter and tobacco, lending a festive air to the occasion celebrating the dead man's journey to a better world. Johnjoe went to the ceremony but was going to leave quickly feeling that he was an outsider. As he was about to go, the widow clawed at him and screamed: "You didn't save my husband. Sure, you hauled in Donald Doherty."

"I'm sorry for your loss, Missus, but his body never resurfaced." Paddy the Pike heard the exchange and intervened: "Sure, Susan, the young man did his best."

The next morning the admiral called Johnjoe to his cottage where Donald was still on the mend. The admiral said, "You were the only one who could have saved my son. I want to give you this Claddagh ring, an heirloom in our family, for you to keep and give to your beloved. It symbolizes love, friendship, and loyalty, all of which you displayed yesterday by risking your life for Donald."

Johnjoe began to protest, but the admiral stopped him, "I'm the King of the Claddagh, and this is my wish."

The ring was heavy, made of gold, embossed with the Claddagh logo—a heart held with two hands, a crown above with the initials "R" on the left, "J" on the right, representing Richard Joyce, the most famous goldsmith in Ireland.

Johnjoe said his thanks. "I have a lass named Mary, and this will be for her."

* * *

At St. Michael's Maureen Linnane was anxious for more candies like the ones Tommy had brought her and her sister Eileen before: creamy butterscotch, chewy caramels, and black licorice. They had melted on her tongue. Tommy had promised his sisters another bag if they could coax from Josie or Nellie where Johnjoe had gone. Maureen thought eleven-year-old Josie was the weak link because she longed to be friends with the other girls. Maureen tried subtlety: "Sure, Josie, they wouldn't tell a little girl like you where Johnjoe was going. That's for adults to know. Maybe your sister Mary because she's almost grown."

"Well, Maureen, if you're so smart, you should know where Johnjoe is. "

"I may not know that, but I'm sure they wouldn't tell a baby like you."

"I'm not a baby," Josie cried. "Johnjoe went off with the Quakers to Galway for fishing."

Just then Mary Mullins walked into the dormitory. Josie turned beet-red and began to weep. Mary knew that her sister had told. Taking her sister in her arms, Mary said, "Don't worry. They'll never find him."

165

Sister Clare heard the commotion and bustled into the room, learning from the Mullins girls what had happened. Because Tommy was the only family his sisters had, Sister Clare couldn't keep him from visiting, but she was determined to be present when he was around to make it as hard as possible for him to learn about Johnjoe.

A week after Tommy had seen his sisters, he came snooping around St. Michael's looking for news about Johnjoe.

"You found out where Johnjoe went," Tommy said.

"I did," Maureen said.

"Well, tell me," Tommy demanded.

"Give us our treats," Maureen said.

"I didn't have any money today."

"No sweets, no news," Maureen said, surprising Tommy with her boldness.

"You little bitch," Tommy said, about to throttle her when Sister Clare flew into the room.

"I thought I smelled trouble, and I was right," Sister Clare said. "Get out."

Tommy left frustrated, but he would keep trying.

* * *

Donald Doherty and Johnjoe were headed out fishing when Siobhan Doherty, Donald's sister, approached Johnjoe. "You've got the ring that was meant for me. I want it back. That's the ring Granny is going to bestow on me when I get married."

Donald was mortified by his sister's words. "But Da gave the ring to him for saving me."

"I don't care," Siobhan said. "It was meant for me."

Johnjoe was nonplussed. "If it belongs to you, I'll give it back."

Smiling at her triumph, Siobhan went to the fish market to help her mother.

The two young men then took a small hooker they had untied from the quay, keeping close to the western shore in sight of the other fishermen in the bay. Turning south, they were searching for cod and ling.

After only a few minutes on the water, Donald saw a brown fin slicing the gray ocean ahead of them. "Johnjoe, a sunfish."

A basking shark had come up from the south attracted by the lone hooker, which might appear to it as another large fish. The young men didn't have enough time to make it back to shore, and the fish was too far away for the other hookers to see and at an angle the watcher on the cliff couldn't catch sight of. They took the sails down and used their oars to reach a partially submerged cave near Doolin, too small for the behemoth to enter. Intrigued, the shark inspected the cave mouth and made circles in the water just outside it, passing back and forth while Donald and Johnjoe watched the fifty feet of blue-black fish troll around them.

The fish was close enough to Johnjoe that he could see that the gill openings of the shark were so large that they extended right around the neck with those of the first pair almost meeting on the throat below. The fish swam on the surface of the water, its mouth open, ingesting hundreds of gallons of water to chew on the plankton and small crustaceans it devoured with its small teeth.

Suddenly the shark shot straight out of the water, heaving its ten tons at the blue sky, then a second time he jumped, and a third, all in a matter of seconds.

"He would have turned our hooker into splinters," said Donald.

"But his breaching wasn't directed at us. We're safe and snug in here."

"But remember how he killed Sammy the Salmon, John."

"Yes, because we stuck a harpoon in his belly. We attacked him."

A second basking shark followed the first. "I'll bet the breaching is some kind of mating ritual," Johnjoe explained to his friend.

"John, our only chance is to wait them out or hope they go into the bay where the other hookers and the watcher will spy them out."

"But, Donald, they're not so much hunting us as following us."

"No matter, one flick of their tails would finish us."

After a few minutes, the sharks turned south, their dorsal fins slicing through the gray water. "God, they're beautiful," Johnjoe said.

"You're daft entirely. That's months of light from the oil in his liver and plenty of shark meat for us," Donald said.

"They're beautiful."

Later that evening, the admiral called Johnjoe to his cottage where a weeping Siobhan stood next to him. The admiral was raging, his eyes burning and his face red. "John," the admiral said, "I gave that ring to you as my daughter well knows. I'm ashamed of her asking for it back."

"Admiral," said Johnjoe, "I've been thinking on this, and I want to cause Siobhan no unhappiness. Your custom of giving the Claddagh ring to a married daughter is holy and sacred. I hope you will permit me to return the ring to you for its proper use. That you thought so well of me to bestow it—is gift enough. Here is the ring," Johnjoe said handing it to the admiral. "By the time I finish my stay here, I may have earned enough from Mr. Todhunter to buy my own ring for my Mary."

Johnjoe's generosity disarmed the admiral. Ready to lash out again at Siobhan, Johnjoe's words stunned him. He walked over to Granny Lydon and gave her the ring for Siobhan. "John, you're a grand man entirely," the admiral said.

Siobhan wasted no time getting the ring. A day later at the festival of Midsummer's Eve, Michael the Mackerel tossed a burning stick at her feet. When she tossed back the stick to him, a marriage was struck. Siobhan gave Michael the Claddagh ring, which he would return to her when the priest solemnized their marriage the next morning. The village would give the couple a new cottage and a boat or a share in one.

The next day Michael was not above a little mischief. As he met Johnjoe on the beach, he took the ring from his pocket and flashed it at him. Johnjoe kicked him in the back of his pants, sent him sprawling face forward onto the sand, and kept walking.

Chapter 20

Still determined to run down Johnjoe, Tommy Linnane saw his chance when one of the men in the Listowel workhouse died of the fever. Father Cavanagh would say the funeral Mass for the man the next morning, and Sister Clare would attend, leaving him an hour or so to snoop around St. Michael's to discover what Maureen had learned about the whereabouts of Johnjoe. He bought a large bag of sweets to tempt his sisters.

To be on the safe side, Tommy waited until all the mourners were in church before he headed for the dormitory.

"You brought our treats," said Maureen as soon as she saw her brother.

Dangling the bag back and forth in front of her face, Tommy said, "Right here, as soon as you tell me what I want to know."

Snatching the bag from her brother, Maureen said, "He traveled to Galway, to the Claddagh, with the Quakers, something about fishing."

"You done good, Maureen. Another bag of sweets next time I come if you can find out any more."

Tommy got away from St. Michael's fast. The information had given him both an opportunity and a challenge. He must learn more before approaching Gray and getting another whipping. When he got to the workhouse, one of the Quakers, Mr. Pim, was helping distribute the stirabout. Tommy approached him. "Sir, I understand some of your religion are fishermen."

"Not really, but we've decided to help the Irish fishermen where we can. We've assisted the people at Ring and Ballycotton, and that's improved things in those places. Now we've moving on to the Claddagh in Galway."

Tommy had acquired some more information, but he wondered if he was ready to face landlord Gray again. After waiting for a few days, Tommy screwed up his courage to approach the man.

Gray lived in a Georgian house of red brick outside Listowel. Formal gardens surrounded the house, and as Tommy walked up, Gray was berating a young farmer working on his rose bushes. "You cut some blossoms, you scut. Cut back only the deadheads, mind. Let the new buds alone." He smashed the boy across the face with his riding crop.

Turning at the sound of the gravel crunching behind him, Gray scowled at Tommy who almost gave up and retreated. "What do you want?" Gray barked.

Twisting his cap in his hand and assuming his most hangdog look, Tommy said, "Sorry to bother you, Mr. Gray, but I think I may have some news of the villain Johnjoe Kevane."

"I hope you're sure, boy, and not wasting my time again."

"My sister at St. Michael's told me that the Quakers took him to the Claddagh village in Galway to work with them on the fishing there."

"Well, that does make some sense," said Gray. "I know those do-gooders are hoping to improve the fisheries if they can get those lazy bastards to work. It also gets the criminal away from the dragoons. Here's a crown for your efforts. I'll write a letter to Mr. Boyle at the workhouse telling him that you're working for me, and I'll fire this fool."

"Yes, Sir."

"Then I want you to come back here, take one of my horses and ride to Dingle. There you'll find Captain Packenham in the barracks and tell him your news. I will give you another crown and a job when you return."

"Yes, Mr. Gray."

Tommy was thrilled, a crown in his pocket, the promise of a job, a horse under him, and a chance to get Johnjoe. He could not want more.

After skirting Tralee, Tommy took the lower road to Dingle, which paralleled the ocean on his left. The ocean and sky were blue and the sun was shining. Three hours of hard riding brought him to Dingle where he sought out the barracks of the dragoons, a building of gray stone sitting atop a hill.

Tommy knocked on the door and found the man with the black patch staring at him. "Captain Packenham, I have word of Johnjoe Kevane. Mr. Gray sent me," Tommy said.

Packenham was startled by the news and grabbed Tommy, "Tell me boy."

"He's with the Quakers at the Claddagh in Galway, Captain."

"He's not in Newfoundland."

"That was a lie to put you off, Sir."

"I thought so. Lieutenant Thomas, we have yet to meet a priest in this country who tells the truth."

The captain handed Tommy a crown.

Tommy said, "The Quakers have some business with the fishing and brought him along."

"I heard the interfering bastards were fooling with the fisheries. Boy, tell Mr. Gray we'll be right after the culprit."

After Tommy left, Packenham and Thomas prepared the troops for the ride to Galway, a new spring in the captain's step. "I can feel it in my water, Lieutenant. The blackguard is there, and we'll hang him in Galway town. Canon Long, the bishop, and all those religious with their lies won't be able to rescue him."

Just as they were ready to leave Dingle, Packenham received a letter from his commanding officer:

Captain Packenham:

Accompany your troops immediately to Cobh where the Queen lands in four days. I will meet you there with my troops from Dublin.

General Penny

Packenham was conflicted. He had his orders, but he also wanted to hang Kevane. Never before had he disobeyed an order from his commander. He rationalized his decision to pursue Kevane by thinking he would be protecting the Queen from a murderer.

When Lieutenant Thomas asked him about the letter, Packenham lied. "In two weeks we're to form part of the guard for the Queen in Dublin."

On their way to Galway, Lieutenant Thomas was increasingly worried about his captain who spoke to no dragoon but him. As they met poor people traveling the roads, Packenham would accost them. "Five pounds to the man who can lead me to Johnjoe Kevane, the murderer of Major Mahon." Each group they ran across received the same query. Thomas had barely been able to rescue the three captured prisoners from torture in the barn after the rebellion. Only the immediate need for Packenham to have his eye patch restored had saved them. Thomas feared for his captain's sanity, the man more isolated, mumbling to himself, less aware of his surroundings. He was living in another world, cut adrift from the suffering of those around him. The black heights of the Cliffs of Moher—with the broad Atlantic pummeling itself against them—was a natural wonder, breathtaking in beauty and majesty. The captain never noticed them.

Thomas knew that the real danger for the dragoons would be the captain's ability to deal with the Claddagh people who had a terrible history with the English, Cromwell's army in the 1650s clearing the Claddagh and Galway of all "Irish and popish inhabitants" and awarding their land to his supporters. In 1649 Cromwell and his

Puritans slaughtered 3,552 inhabitants of Drogheda and 2000 more in Wexford.

Gradually the Claddagh people had reclaimed their land, but harbored deep hatred for the Protestant marauders who had even sailed thirty miles west to the Aran Islands to kill more Irish Catholics. Renowned for their hostility to outsiders, especially the authorities, 200 hardy Claddagh fishermen were more than a match for six dragoons even though armed—if Packenham would incite a skirmish. These were not the listless paupers the captain terrorized on the roads.

Thomas knew also that Packenham would not bring the youth back to Dingle for trial. Cut loose from all civilian authority, the captain would exercise summary justice there. His captain reminded Thomas of the tigers they saw in the jungles of the Punjab, ferocious and wild, doing what they pleased.

Outside the village of Doolin close to Galway town, the dragoons met another motley assemblage making their way to the workhouse. Stopping the group, Packenham repeated his offer. "Five pounds to the man who can help me capture Johnjoe Kevane, the murderer of Major Mahon."

One middle-aged farmer shouted back, "I suppose you'll hang him."

"Of course," replied Packenham.

"As if you haven't murdered enough of us yet," the farmer yelled back.

Before Lieutenant Thomas could intervene, Packenham charged at the man and slashed his face with his riding crop screaming, "No wonder this country is in such a state when you protect murderers." The man stood unflinching in front of Packenham's gray horse, the other people in the group sliding to the side of the road. The man bore his bloody cut defiantly and shouted, "You're the reason we're in such a sorry condition, eating us out of house and home and driving us from our land."

Lieutenant Thomas rode up and got between the farmer and Packenham who was prepared to strike out at the man again. "Captain, we're almost to the Claddagh. Let's pursue our criminal."

* * *

In Galway the admiral had agreed to a trial of three months for a trawler, the *Vivid*, so long as it didn't enter the bay. The Quakers had imported a captain, Arthur Chard, from Falmouth, Cornwall, at Quaker expense because of his skill as a deep-water fisherman. Todhunter, Johnjoe, and Donald Doherty also were on board the ship, Johnjoe as translator for the Englishmen who knew no Irish.

Trouble erupted immediately as the Claddagh men were opposed to where Chard wished to drop anchor and lower their nets. Johnjoe spent his time interceding with the Claddagh men to follow the captain's orders. The results were mixed. The *Vivid* made a fine catch of cod, but the rocky bottom of the sea fouled and destroyed many of the nets. When the *Vivid* brought the catch just outside the bay, hookers went out to bring it to shore.

"Sure, we told them not to cast the nets near the western shore," Donald said. "But what do we know only living here all our lives."

Johnjoe said, "At least we caught some fish."

Some of the fish were brought to market; the rest, to a newly established curing house.

Though the initial use of the trawler was not very encouraging, the Quakers were determined to keep at it through a trial of several months.

* * *

When the dragoons had reached the town of Galway, Packenham asked one of the townspeople where the Claddagh was. The man pointed to a cluster of thatched, beehive stone cottages on the southwestern tip of the shore. The dragoons found only barefoot women and children on the beach hunting for baitfish or mending nets on a grassy area close by. Dressed in blue coats and red petticoats, the women stood in stark contrast to the gray water of the bay and the blue-black clouds scudding towards them. The women and children paid the dragoons no mind until Packenham grabbed and shook a young woman with black hair, a terrified child clinging to her side.

"See here, Miss, I'm looking for a young man by the name of Johnjoe Kevane," said Packenham. Confused by his English because she spoke only Irish, she stood trembling before him. Misinterpreting her lack of response as resistance, Packenham grabbed her arm so fiercely he left the imprints of his fingers when Lieutenant Thomas scurried over. "Captain, she speaks no English."

Frustrated by his need for a translator, Packenham sent Lieutenant Thomas into Galway town to find someone who knew both Irish and English. Thomas returned with an innkeeper who asked the woman about Johnjoe. She answered that no Johnjoe Kevane was living in the Claddagh, but other Irishmen and Englishmen whom she didn't know were working aboard the trawler just outside Galway Bay.

Some miles out in the bay the winds were whipping the water into a frenzy, black clouds rolling towards them. From the shore the dragoons could see the *Vivid* taking aboard men from the hookers and tying the boats to the trawler. Other hookers were making for land propelled by the furious winds. The storm was almost on them, churning the surf into green waves topped with foam.

"I want to go to that trawler now," Packenham insisted, "no matter how rough the seas." The translator intervened with the woman the captain had accosted.

"Sure, the storm is driving the hookers to shore, Sir. No one will go out in this," the woman said. With that, thunder and lightning cracked the purple sky. The men in the boats handed their catch to their waiting wives while they raced their boats by hand to the quay to be fastened and then turned upside down to avoid the rain pelting the beach. The fishermen paid no attention to the dragoons, pretending they didn't exist because the troops meant only trouble. The families all ran to their cottages out of the storm, leaving only Packenham and his men drenched on the beach. Packenham burned with anger, but like King Lear with the storm crashing about him, he could do nothing about the elements.

For the moment, Packenham and his sodden men headed for the town, where an inn, The Whale's Head, offered a fire, a meal, and a place to stay. They would remain at the inn for the night until the storm blew itself out.

The next morning was sun-filled, and Packenham bristled to meet the admiral and get out to the trawler. Packenham and Lieutenant Thomas walked to the admiral's cottage, the translator in tow. Packenham knocked at the cottage door that Mrs. Doherty opened.

"Good morning, Sirs," she said.

Packenham said, "We wish to speak with the admiral."

"He's out fishing, Sir."

"When he returns, tell him I want to speak with him immediately."

Of course, the admiral had learned of the visit from the dragoons and the reason for it. He would give nothing away, especially if it was to protect the life of the young man who had saved his son.

Later that afternoon when the hookers had returned, Packenham, Thomas, and the translator raced to the beach as the admiral's hooker landed. The admiral invited them to his cottage where they sat at the wooden kitchen table.

"I'm hunting a young man Johnjoe Kevane, and it will go hard for anyone who is shielding him," Packenham said.

Before the captain could proceed, the admiral said, "You put violent hands on our woman."

Packenham had the grace to be embarrassed. "I thought she was

177

making a fool of me. I didn't know she had no English. I apologize for my rudeness."

Mollified, the admiral replied, "We have no one here by that name."

"He could be on the trawler anchored outside the bay," said the captain.

"A mixed crew of Englishmen and Irishmen are aboard. I don't know them all, except for my son and a Quaker, Mr. Todhunter," said the admiral.

"At first light tomorrow, I want to go to that ship and inspect it personally," Packenham said.

"I'll take you myself," said the admiral.

Later that evening, just before dusk, when the dragoons had returned to their inn, two hookers manned by the admiral and three veteran Claddagh fisherman set out for the *Vivid*. The admiral's visit surprised Captain Chard. "You're out here late."

"Captain, I need to have a private word with John Kavanagh."

The two found a cubbyhole on deck in which to talk, the sunset casting rose light on the water. "A Captain Packenham and dragoons have come to the village to seek you out," the admiral said. "He called you "Johnjoe Kevane," not John Kavanagh as we know you, so I truthfully denied knowing anyone of that name. When he demanded to be taken out to the ship tomorrow morning, I thought it was better to agree than to arouse his suspicions. He didn't tell us why he's after you, but of this I'm sure, he means you no good."

"Some day, please God, I'll tell you my story. Packenham's a cold bastard, Admiral, hunting me for months. I'll have to hide from him out here on the trawler."

"I have an idea," said the admiral. "I'm going to leave an extra hooker tied to the trawler. If Packenham comes near you, Donald and you take the hooker and head for the open water. I'll make sure he never reaches you. I'll have a word with Mr. Todhunter and Captain Chard about our plan but not the reasons for it."

At dawn with Lieutenant Thomas and the translator with him, Packenham paced up and down on the quay reading his Bible and waiting for the admiral.

Just as they were ready to jump off in the admiral's hooker, the watcher on the cliffs let out a yell and the red petticoats flew on the rope from the gables. The entire village erupted into life, some men running for their boats while others tied the chains and cable with its harpoon to the boulder, and then ran the weapon of death down to the spearman to carry off in his boat.

A dazed Packenham stood by as Claddagh men raced by them to set their hookers afloat.

"They've sighted a sunfish, a basking shark," said the interpreter, as ten hookers loaded with men carrying ropes and knives shot into the green surf.

"I want to go to the trawler right now," Packenham insisted, shaking his kirpan at the admiral.

"We'll have time for that," the admiral said.

Lieutenant Thomas yelled to his superior, "Patrick, this is dangerous. We're not sea-faring men."

"I've chased that murdering bastard for two years now. It's all I think of. I'll have him today," Packenham yelled.

All the hookers cut through the foaming surf, rowing back towards the shark. The men in the trawler had also spotted the shark swimming on the surface and began to head for it. From the trawler, Donald and Johnjoe watched intently.

Despite himself, Packenham became caught up in the fever of the chase. "Get closer," screamed Packenham as he drew the kirpan from the scabbard at his side. The sight of the sleek blue-black monster inflamed him. Like the maddened Ahab seeking Moby Dick, he screamed at the giant shark, "I'll hack you to bits and do the same to Kevane."

Led by the spearman, the admiral's hooker churned the green water into foam as it neared the monster swimming lazily on the surface, indifferent to those who would kill it. The spearman approached within a few yards of the shark and plunged his harpoon into the gray streak under the big fin, triggering an eruption of blood, foam, and sea as the fish twisted away from the source of its agony. The cable tightened as the fish submerged into the depths of the ocean. A few seconds later the sea blew open as the shark broke the surface, leaped high in the air, and then landed on the admiral's boat, its ten tons crushing it, and driving Packenham, Thomas, the spearman, and the admiral into the deep.

Preparing to head for the open water, Donald and Johnjoe had untied their hooker when they saw the red-jacketed dragoons in the admiral's boat with its white sails crushed by the shark. Instead of fleeing from Packenham, Donald and Johnjoe changed course and rowed to rescue the admiral and the men in his hooker. Packenham came to the surface and saw Johnjoe whom he recognized immediately. The two locked eyes, and Packenham screamed, "I've got you." Then the green waters engulfed him.

Lieutenant Thomas, the spearman, and the admiral resurfaced where the other boats could haul them in, but as the fish turned and twisted away, it wrapped the cable around itself and Packenham. In an instant Johnjoe decided to save his tormentor as if he could atone for his shooting of Major Mahon. He swam towards Packenham and the shark to free his enemy from the cable, the captain staring at him wild-eyed with hate the full time. Unable to extend his arms fully because of the cable, Packenham tried to stab Johnjoe with his kirpan. He jabbed at Johnjoe once, twice, with his sword, slashing the young man's left arm. Because the cable was slippery from blood and water, Johnjoe couldn't loosen it, all the while trying to evade the thrusts of Packenham's kirpan and keep his breath by bobbing up and down in the water.

With a glanciing swipe of his tail, the shark drove Johnjoe underwater where he had to dive deep to avoid the cable that would shackle him in death to the fish and to Packenham. Looking up through the green water illuminated by the sun above, Johnjoe watched the cable swinging to and fro in the ocean currents. In his mind's eye, he saw his mother and father and Mary. He wouldn't let the ocean become his graveyard, but he had to avoid the cable that would bind him to the great fish, a blow from the shark's tail that could finish him, and a strike from the captain's sword. He wanted one more attempt to free Packenham.

As Johnjoe swam toward his nemesis, foam and blood clouded his vision. Packenham stabbed at him again, narrowly missing his throat. "You don't want to be saved," Johnjoe screamed as he treaded water, swimming upright to save his breath.

"I want you dead," Packenham yelled over the roar of the waves and the thrashing of the shark. Johnjoe had had enough. He had tried, so he kicked himself away from Packenham, dislodging the sword and leaving his enemy to the fate he had chosen for himself. The nearest hooker hauled Johnjoe in.

The ocean waters surging over him, Packenham had only one chance—if the shark would swim on the surface. Instead, the shark broke the water briefly, Packenham stuck like a limpet to its side. Sputtering water and foam, Packenham cried, "Oh God, my rock and my salvation." Then the beast dove for a run out to sea. In the green water, Packenham saw his own air bubbles escaping from him, his last conscious thought, "I won't get him."

As Donald, the spearman, the admiral and Thomas rowed to shore, the lieutenant cried out, "Captain Packenham is missing." He had seen Johnjoe's efforts to untangle the cable.

A half hour later after the shark swam itself out in the open sea, the boulder in the cleft of the mountain stopped dancing, and the hookers returned to shore to help the villagers pull the behemoth in. Frantic, Lieutenant Thomas begged the admiral, "Please, Sir, send a hooker out to search for the captain. I'll go with them."

A collective moan, an anguished keening, rose from the men, women, and children pulling the monster to land. The people shuddered to see the body of a man in a tattered red uniform, wedded in death to the great fish by the cable wrapped several times around them both. Bleached white by the salt of the sea, the captain was a ghost, stripped of his eye patch, his scar and empty eye socket exposed for all to see, his arms akimbo like the crucified Christ. His Victoria medal still clung to the scraps of his red jacket. Thomas would make sure to pin the medal to a new jacket for his burial, the captain's arms folded over it.

"Good Jesus, poor Patrick," Lieutenant Thomas said as he drew his saber on shore to cut the cable that tied his superior to his death.

"Just a minute, Sir. You'll not cut the cable. That's our lifeline to the sunfish," said a fisherman. "We're sorry for your man, but you'll wait until we unwind the ropes and cable." Instead of objecting, Thomas helped the fishermen uncoil the cable from around the shark and his friend's body. The hero of Modkree to end this way: drowned by being yoked to a shark. Thomas gently carried the body to the beach and laid it on a blanket. With the translator along, Thomas went to the admiral and asked that some woman from the Claddagh wash the salt-rimed corpse and make a black eye patch to cover the scar. He asked also that a coffin be made and gave the admiral money for these tasks.

"Admiral," Thomas said, "this man was a hero in India. His wound scarred his spirit as well as his body, but I want to treat him with dignity. He deserves that. We'll put a new uniform on him and bring him back to be buried with his people in Roscommon."

The admiral nodded agreement.

"On a different subject, Admiral," Thomas said, "tell Kevane I'm going to report that he died at sea while the captain chased him. Hunting him has caused only death. I'll pursue him no further, and I want him to know that. As far as the dragoons are concerned, he is dead. But he still has enemies in Listowel, Gray, a landowner and his informant. Kevane will have to find some way to deal with them.

Also, he should avoid Dingle where he's known. Thank you for these courtesies for my captain."

One of the women in the village cleaned and sewed up Johnjoe's wound from the captain's sword. When the admiral told him what Lieutenant Thomas had said, Johnjoe replied, "I've learned to rejoice over no man's death, but Packenham was a heartless bastard. I feel like I've escaped from jail. God bless Lieutenant Thomas. He has given me a new life."

* * *

In 1850 the fish market suffered terribly because the poor could not pay for the fish. The Quaker efforts to revive the fishing industry in the Claddagh had mixed results. After spending three months on the trawler, Todhunter sadly admitted that "we landsmen begin to find there is more difficulty in successful fishing than we supposed and now wonder that the poor half-starved and discouraged Irish fisheries have fallen below the expectations of some of their warm but not judicious patrons." For specifics, the trawler the Quakers had purchased couldn't handle the heavy Irish seas and the English nets they used were too light.

Todhunter went on to say that the character of the coast was "so rocky and foul within sounds for trawling" that fishing was dangerous and futile. It was true, Todhunter said, that "fish did pass along the coast at specific seasons, but the rocky sea bottom of the west and south-west coasts did not provide the fish with the nutrients to feed them consistently."

After more than a year in the Claddagh, the Quakers had redeemed hookers from pawn and had gotten the village back fishing. They had taught the village how to cure their catch and how to catch lobster and deep-sea shrimp.

As for Johnjoe, Todhunter paid him fifteen pounds for his work, much of which he spent on buying a Claddagh ring for Mary

Mullins from a jeweler the admiral recommended. He left for St. Michael's and Listowel.

*   *   *

Two days later *The Freeman's Journal* reported the drowning at sea of Captain Packenham of the Queen's Light Dragoons and the suspect he was pursuing, Johnjoe Kevane. When Father Cavanagh read the news, he cried. He went over to the school and told Sister Clare who burst into tears. "We'll have to tell the girls," the priest said.

"I'll tell them, Father, but it will be a heartbreak."

As it happened, Sister Clare didn't have to be the messenger of bad news. Gray had read the story and told Tommy who was ecstatic. Now he could have Mary all to himself. Tommy made a beeline to St. Michael's where he evaded Sister Clare and found the girls in the knitting room.

"Well, Mary, Johnjoe has gotten what he deserved, dead from drowning in Galway Bay being chased by the dragoons."

Mary, Josie, and Nellie broke into sobs. Mary ran to Sister Clare to confirm the news, but the look on her face was enough. "Mary, I'm sorry," the nun said and hugged her.

Mary said, "First me Ma and Da and now this. I can't stand it."

*   *   *

Tommy had enough sense to leave Mary alone for a couple of days. When he next visited St. Michael's, he told Mary, "I'm Mr. Gray's middle man, and he has given me a farm which I'm moving into soon. It's not every man who can offer you that. I need a wife, and I'm asking for your hand. Think about it, and I'll be back in a few days for your answer." When he grabbed her roughly for a kiss, she slapped him.

"I wouldn't marry you if you were the last man on earth."

"You'd better change your mind, Mary, or you'll end up like your parents—poor as church mice."

Mary listened to Tommy but knew she didn't love him. She then went to Sister Clare for advice. She knew the nun cared for her and her sisters and was practical.

"Mary, you've got to follow your heart. If you love Tommy, marry him. If you don't, wait until you find the right man. You'll know."

Chapter 21

State Drawing Room at Dublin Castle.
Reception in St Patrick's Hall, Dublin Castle on the occasion of Queen
Victoria's visit to Ireland in August, 1849.

The Illustrated London News, 11 August 1849.

multitext.ucc.ie/viewgallery/219?slideshow=10 -

While Johnjoe was in Galway, Queen Victoria, Prince Albert, and
their six children landed at Cobh, which she renamed "Queenstown"
in honor of her visit. The Queen had donated 2,000 pounds for
Famine relief. Security was a worry for her trip. In May of 1848,
an Irishman from Adare, County Limerick, had fired a pistol at the
Queen as she rode in her carriage on Constitution Hill in London. But
Victoria was unharmed. Later some crazed Irish patriots hatched a plot
to kidnap the Queen and hold her hostage in the Wicklow Mountains.

When Irish patriot Charles Gavan Duffy learned of the conspiracy, he warned the planners that it was hopeless because 10,000 British dragoons stood ready in Dublin. In any event only 200 volunteers mustered for the supposed kidnapping, and the plot died stillborn.

Because Victoria never traveled to the interior or to the west of Ireland where the Famine had hit the hardest, she never saw the plight of poor cottiers like the Kevanes tumbled from homes and driven from the country. The poor encapsulated their feelings about her visit in a piece of doggerel: "Arise ye dead of Skibbereen and come to Cork to see the Queen."

*   *   *

The next time Tommy came to see Mary, he insisted that she marry him. "Mary, I have a job and land. I need to know what your intentions are toward me. Plenty other women in Listowel would have me, you know."

"Marry one of them then. I won't."

"You had better change your mind, Mary. Johnjoe is dead."

"I won't marry you."

*   *   *

With the dragoons no longer hounding him, Johnjoe walked to Listowel in a day going through Ennis and Gort, then taking the ferry across the Shannon to Tarbert, carrying the Claddagh ring that he hoped to bestow on Mary Mullins. Sister Clare and Father Cavanagh were in the kitchen talking when Johnjoe walked in.

"Good God," said the priest.

"Jesus, Mary, and Joseph," a rare oath from Sister Clare.

"Yes, it's me," said Johnjoe, bigger, stronger, and red-faced from sun and wind.

They exchanged tears and hugs.

187

"We read that you had drowned after being chased by the dragoons," said Father Cavanagh.

"That was the kindness of Lieutenant Thomas to clear my name. My only worries are Gray and Tommy."

"We'll talk about them later," Father Cavanagh said. "You better see some girls upstairs first."

Johnjoe sprinted upstairs where the first person to see him was Mary who shrieked "Johnjoe" and threw herself into his arms, dropping her knitting on the floor. Once Mary recovered, she yelled at Johnjoe, "Not a word from you these last two years. You could at least have sent a letter or message that you were still alive. And that terrible Tommy Linnane telling us you were drowned and pestering me to marry him. He's become Gray's gombeen man, lording it over the tenants. I love you, but I'm furious with you."

Dumbstruck, Johnjoe gathered himself to plead with her. "But, Mary, the dragoons followed me everywhere to hang me. I had to run from them or die."

"You could not write even once."

Johnjoe pulled Mary to him and kissed her. She responded by throwing her knitting basket at him. He gave up, limping down the stairs. Some welcome.

*   *   *

In the years Johnjoe was away, Gray had become the largest landowner in Listowel, what the Irish derisively called a "landgrabber," buying up more and more of the properties of his cottier tenants who couldn't pay rent. Because he and his wife were childless, Gray focused all his energy on becoming rich. He owned hundreds of sheep and forty cows. Tommy Linnane grew into the perfect gombeen man for Gray: mean, bad-tempered, and avaricious. Linnane relished the power he held over the cottiers, accompanied by the dragoons as he tore down hovel after hovel.

One of the larger plots of land Gray and Linnane had their eyes on was owned by Peter Wilson who feared no one. Linnane had given the man notice that he and his family would be evicted, drawing only a scoff from him.

"You'll not tear down my house, shrimpeen—that is, if you want to keep breath in you."

Linnane reported the man's threat to Gray who itched to see the man grovel. The following morning Gray and Linnane rode with four dragoons to Wilson's cottage, high on a hill with lush pastureland below. Gray was licking his chops. The night before, one of the destructives had warned Wilson that the tumbling was scheduled for the next morning. In their red jackets the dragoons would stand by and watch another cottage being destroyed.

Linnane banged on the door: "Open up and clear out. 'Tis time." When no response came, Linnane had two of his workers use a battering ram to cave in the door. No one was inside, but the table, chairs and beds were still in place, even a fire burning in the hearth. Though puzzled, Linnane decided to start the work of destruction, lighting a firebrand from the hearth. Running back outside, Linnane raised the burning torch to ignite the thatched roof. Two shots rang out. A bullet just missed Tommy, and Gray was shot off his horse dead, falling into the barnyard mud. Stunned, the dragoons didn't know which way to charge because the firing had come from two different directions. The dragoons rode to the top of the hill, but could see no one. The marksmen had done their jobs well, killing the landlord while leaving the Queen's soldiers untouched. No tumbling would take place this day. And Tommy was out of a job, having made enemies even with Gray's wife and all the other farmers.

As for the Wilsons, they were on their way to Cobh for passage to America. They had held back their rent to pay their way to freedom and had gotten rid of the landlord all in one stroke.

Although with Gray's death Tommy had lost his job, Mary Mullins wouldn't know that yet. He would see her and demand she marry him immediately. Riding Gray's horse, Tommy made his way to St. Michael's and was shocked to see a familiar figure with two sheep dogs driving the herd toward the river—Johnjoe. The bastard wasn't dead. Furious, Tommy wanted to rid himself of his enemy once and for all. Tommy dismounted, took Gray's rifle from its scabbard, and led the horse through the field trailing after Johnjoe whose back was to him. Tying the horse to a gorse bush, Tommy saw that Johnjoe had walked along the bank near the river, still facing away from him, the sheep grazing on the ground above.

It started to rain, the spattering of the drops on trees and leaves muffling the sound of Tommy's footsteps. Johnjoe had moved about twenty yards away and below him, his back an inviting target. Nobody would see Tommy shoot, and he could get away clean. With Johnjoe gone, he would have Mary all to himself.

Tommy raised and aimed his musket when a rabbit spooked his horse, drawing the attention of Johnjoe and his dogs that ran at the intruder. Johnjoe saw it all in an instant—Tommy was going to murder him—after all he had suffered to be killed by this villain. When the dogs jumped at him, Tommy misfired, the shot high and wide, hitting Johnjoe in the shoulder and spinning him around. Turning to face his enemy, Johnjoe said, "You'd shoot me in the back, dirty coward. You were always no good."

While Johnjoe staggered toward him holding his right arm, Tommy reloaded while fending off the two dogs. "Now I'm going to finish you off face to face and put a ball into your chest as you did to Major Mahon. Then I'll marry Mary."

"Never."

Using his musket to keep off the dogs, Tommy raised his gun

when one of the dogs leaped and bit his hand, the rifle flying down the bank below. Scrambling to recover his gun, Tommy slipped on the wet grass and fell headfirst down the bank into the river. Enraged, Johnjoe stumbled after Tommy. With his one good arm, he grabbed the musket.

Johnjoe thought of shooting Tommy, but wanted no more killings on his soul. "Get up, you bastard, or I'll put a ball into your carcass." Grabbing him by the hair with his one good hand, he saw Tommy's brains leak red and gray from his smashed forehead and plop into the water, his skull crushed by the boulder he had landed on.

Johnjoe vomited.

Johnjoe stumbled to St. Michael's, the dogs driving the sheep home. When Mary saw all the blood, she screamed. "What happened?"

"Tommy." Then he fainted.

Johnjoe later woke in the dormitory with a sling on his arm.

Sister Clare explained, "The ball went clean through. In two weeks you'll be as fit as ever." Mary was hovering beside her.

Johnjoe said, "Tell Father Cavanagh to fetch the sheriff. Tommy's lying in the river, his head smashed against a rock."

In the twilight the priest and the sheriff found Tommy's body. The horse was still tied to the bush, the fired musket lying in the mud on the bank. Tying a cloth around Tommy's head to hold it together, the two men lifted the body up the bank and draped it over Gray's horse.

"He was a bad actor, about to commit murder," Father Cavanagh said. "May God have mercy on his soul."

"He misfired, thank God, or else he would have done for your man," the sheriff said. "I feel sorry for his sisters."

"Don't," the priest said. "He was never any good to them anyway. Well, we'll say a Mass for him and pray that the Lord will be more merciful to him in death than Tommy was in life."

* * *

Once Mary was certain of Johnjoe's return to good health, she was determined to make him suffer for abandoning them. When he was feeding and cooling the horse in the barn one day, Mary went out to him, yelling, "Johnjoe, I am supposed to fall into your arms just because you've returned. You might up and leave again. You left us once."

Johnjoe took off the horse's saddle and rubbed the place underneath to get the blood flowing again. He turned to face Mary.

"No, I'm here to stay, no more running from the dragoons."

"You were supposed to be our older brother. No older brother would leave his loved ones for months and not a peep out of him."

Johnjoe checked the horse's legs for any bruises or bumps and looked at each foot to check for stones.

"But, Mary, I was running from the dragoons who wanted to hang me. They chased me over half of Ireland. Sure, the Claddagh admiral had to hide me on a trawler in Galway Bay."

"You were wonderful with us when Da was going and we came here. But then you were off for months and months, not even one word from you."

"But, Mary, Tommy was an informer, telling Mr. Gray and the dragoons that I had gone to the Claddagh. And then I come home only to have Tommy shoot me."

Mary blushed. "That was our fault. Tommy's sister wheedled the information from Josie."

"Packenham wanted to hang me."

"That's as may be, Johnjoe, but you can't begin courting me as if you'd never left. And I have Josie and Nellie to mother and care for, not just go off on a whim."

"That was no whim. They wanted me in a noose. You're an awful woman, Mary Mullins, to treat me like this. I've come from Galway to buy a farm and marry you, but you have set your face against me."

"You don't even pay attention to me right now. All you care about is Father Cavanagh's horse."

"That's because the horse makes more sense than you."

"Many more men are around here to marry than you. Men who won't up and leave."

"And more colleens to choose from than you who don't spend all their time scolding their men."

Mary turned and rushed across the road to her room and then cried into her knitting.

Johnjoe took the pitchfork and hurled it into a bale of hay.

Father Cavanagh ambled into the barn to use his horse. "I think I caught the tail end of a lover's spat."

"I found little love in it, Father."

Father Cavanagh chuckled. "Shakespeare said, 'The course of true love never did run smooth.' And in my experience the man had it right. Be patient with her, lad."

Mary Mullins had lost both parents, caring for them in their last agony. At sixteen she became mother to Josie and Nellie. When Johnjoe entered her life, he had been a Godsend, he and Brother Leonard sharing the deathwatch with her and guiding the girls at St. Michael's. But then he left abruptly, throwing her back once more on her own resources, the man she had dreamed of marrying. She saw the captain with the black eye patch and sensed his cruelty; and though Father Cavanagh and Sister Clare had explained why Johnjoe had to flee, his departure still stung.

Devastated by Mary's rejection, Johnjoe sought the advice of Sister Clare at work in the kitchen. "Sister, I even brought a Claddagh ring to win her, and she ate the face off me."

"Her parents had just died when you came into her life. Then you left and she thought you were dead. Win her back slowly. Have her read your diary before you give it to Mr. Bewley. She has no idea of what you've suffered. Give her time; she'll come around. She's endured so much loss in her life."

193

Comforted by these words, Johnjoe continued to work for Father Cavanagh and hired himself out to several local farmers to accumulate some savings. He also looked out for a small farm and cottage he could buy for himself and Mary—if she would change her mind and have him.

*　*　*

As Mary read the diary, the suffering of the people aboard the *Ajax* horrified her, especially Johnjoe and his family:

August 3

I was inspired by the priest and overcame my fear to hold Ma's hand once he had to help others. She could no longer speak and tried to push me away but was too weak. I leaned over and kissed Ma and Da on the forehead. After a time Ma's grip relaxed, and she too was gone. I was too numb to cry. Once the mistress saw I wouldn't leave my parents, she moved on to help the little ones, many of whom were now orphans.

Dr. Douglas could find no man willing to bring up the bodies of Ma and Da for fear of the fever—even for a shilling for each body. Finally, two sailors agreed to impale the bodies on a harpoon, Ma and Da together, on the same shaft, and pull them up from their deathbeds in the hold. They were nearly naked, like Christ on the Cross, bleeding water and blood from the Roman centurion's lance.

Once the sailors had the bodies on deck, they put ropes around them and lowered them into a rowboat. They pulled the harpoon from me Ma and Da, and put it in a cauldron of boiling water to sterilize it. Using the ropes, the sailors dumped the bodies into a wooden wagon pulled by a gray horse and driven by a nervous young man.

Father Moylan returned to the ship and took me on a small

rowboat to shore to get me out of the contagion. Dr. Douglas had passed me that morning. After the boat reached shore, I ran to the cart to kiss and hug Ma and Da one last time, but Father Moylan held me back: "I heard your mother, Johnjoe. She wants you to live."

In the wagon were other bodies, some from different ships. Father Moylan and I followed the cart half a mile down to the western end of the island to a pit already filled with dozens of corpses. The driver took the wagon to the edge of the pit and tipped it, so all the bodies fell in together like clods of turf. I was scared, hurt, and angry by turns. My Ma and Da didn't deserve this. My mind flashed back to Major Mahon. Even though he was 3,000 miles away, he was a killer.

After giving her his diary, Johnjoe began to notice a softening in Mary. He had never told her of the horrors of the coffin ships and of Grosse Ile. She was shocked when she read of his shooting of Major Mahon, but she understood why he had done it. From the diary, she saw a new Johnjoe, hunted by the dragoons for his crime but who did good wherever he ran—Skibbereen, Cork, and the Claddagh. Mary read out of sight of Johnjoe, sharing her feelings only with Sister Clare who acknowledged that he had done a terrible deed but that he had confessed his sin and changed his life.

"He killed a man, Sister," Mary said.

"Yes, Mary, but that man may have deserved killing for the hundreds he murdered on his coffin ships, (may God forgive me for saying it)."

"But I don't know if I can love a man who has killed."

"Mary, look here to me. Soldiers have killed and their wives still love them. Trust your eyes and heart. He will make a good husband and father. If you don't want him, someone else will."

After finishing reading the diary, one afternoon Mary came to Johnjoe sitting on a stool as he sheared sheep in the shade of Father

Cavanagh's barn, goldfinches with their yellow wings spread-eagled against the blue sky. Mary sat on a bale of hay. "You killed a man."

"Yes."

A lone skylark warbled its sweet song, getting louder as it climbed.

"I suppose you feel guilty about it."

For a moment, Johnjoe lived in another world, his eyes focused in the distance but not seeing. "Sometimes it gives me nightmares. I'm standing on the Garfinney Bridge in the twilight. When Mahon charged me on his horse, I shot him. But I also saw in my mind's eye the bodies of my Ma and Da awash in blood and tied with a rope to the spear that hauled them from the hold of our ship. They dangled above the blue waters of the St. Lawrence before being dropped into the rowboat that would carry them to shore. I wanted to die. Later, I confessed the murder to Canon Long and did two months penance."

Mary got up from her seat and stood to face Johnjoe. "Sister Clare told me that soldiers kill in battle and their wives still love them."

"I wish I had that excuse, but I don't. My war was personal. I have other nightmares of me Ma and Da being thrown into a mass grave. I killed that man for revenge."

"And how do you feel now, Johnjoe?"

"I'm sorry for the sin, but not that he's dead, if that makes any sense. Christ has forgiven me. I hope you will too."

Holding his hand, Mary said, "Sure, Johnjoe you can't print the diary the way it is."

"And why not?" Johnjoe bristled.

"Because you're indicting yourself as the murderer of Major Mahon."

"But that's what happened, Mary."

"You fool, you would be admitting to the dragoons you killed the man."

"Yes, you're right. I was so anxious to tell my story truthfully that I didn't think of the consequences."

"If I were to marry, I don't want it to be to a dead man. I want a life together. Ask Sister Clare and get her opinion about including the shooting in your book."

"A good idea."

Johnjoe found Sister Clare alone bustling about in the kitchen: "Sister, I need your advice. Should I keep the account of my killing of Major Mahon in the diary when it's printed?"

"Good God, no, Johnjoe. You'd be giving the English a reason to hang you. I thought you had enough sense to leave that out before giving the diary to Mr. Bewley. Besides, your story is powerful enough without it."

"Sister, you're right. Mary said the same, that she didn't want to marry a dead man."

"Well, that's good news entirely. You're both coming to your senses."

In September when Bewley delivered his next load of corn and rice, Johnjoe handed his diary to him. He had omitted the shooting of the major. "This is the story of my life on a coffin ship, Mr. Bewley. I would like you to keep it in your care and publish it if you think it worthy. It's a testimony to my parents, so it's especially important to me that you safeguard it."

"We'll give it a good reading, Johnjoe."

*   *   *

The next day, a Sunday, Johnjoe went to Mary: "I would like to take the girls and you for a buggy ride to Tralee. It would be a change of scenery, like."

"I suppose," Mary answered. Josie and Nellie were thrilled.

Tralee Bay was beautiful, extending around the city like a horseshoe, Mt. Brandon and the Slieve Mish Mountains hovering in the distance.

On their outing, Johnjoe bought a bouquet of flowers from a street seller in Tralee.

Mary said, "I imagine the flowers are for some new colleen who's caught your eye."

"I thought we'd stop at the graves of your Ma and Da and lay them there."

When they came to the "Famine cemetery," as it was now called, the three girls and Johnjoe were alone. Johnjoe was surprised that the girls found the Mullins' gravesite easily enough. "We've come here every Sunday since you've been gone," Mary said. The girls had weeded the site and cleared it of thorns and thistles. The cemetery was bleak, the ground uneven, burial stones turned every which way, like an old man's mouth full of broken teeth.

"Divide the flowers among yourselves," Johnjoe said.

Then they all knelt on the ground after the girls reverently placed the flowers at the head of the grave. The girls and Johnjoe wept.

"When we get some money together," Johnjoe said, "we'll buy a proper head stone for them."

Josie spoke up: "Johnjoe, you've been nothing but kind to us, even if you did desert us for a time."

"I would love to be laying flowers for my own Ma and Da pitched into a mass grave 3000 miles away in Canada. At least you're able to come here to visit. You have each other—and you have me."

Mary walked over to Johnjoe, putting her arm through his and kissing him on the lips: "I love you, Johnjoe. I know I've been cold to you. I've been so afraid to lose you again."

"Never."

'I'm yours if you'll have me," Mary said.

"I will indeed."

When they had returned to St. Michael's, Johnjoe brought a golden Claddagh ring from his purse and handed it to Mary: "I want to marry you and be yours forever. We'll provide for Josie and Nellie, no sending them away." Mary cried at the beauty of the golden ring and kissed Johnjoe, whispering, "I love you."

Father Cavanagh married Mary and Johnjoe, who both wanted

many children, but not before he had bought a good-sized farm in Listowel, one that contained a second cottage for Josie and Nellie. Like an older brother, Johnjoe made sure that the men they married were good and hard working.

*   *   *

After ten years, Johnjoe returned to Dingle and Ballyristeen. He recognized no one. Canon Long was dead, and when Johnjoe knocked at the monastery door, the brother who welcomed him said that Brother Leonard was safe and happy at Mt. Cashel orphanage in St. John's, Newfoundland. Turning up Spa Road, Johnjoe rode the two miles to his old cottage, Mt. Brandon and Conor Pass high above him. Only blackened stones marked where he grew up, but Dingle Bay still glimmered a mile away.

Johnjoe brought with him some tools and two planks of wood, which he formed into a cross and dug into the turf beside the ruins where he had buried his dog. In the wood he carved "The home of Mary and John Kevane, two loving parents." He knelt down and prayed for his parents beneath the cross. It was now that he wished that his parents were buried with their ancestors in Garfinney Cemetery half a mile away.

He thought fleetingly of making a trip to Grosse Ile with Mary and their children to pray at the mass grave, but knew he could not relive those horrors. The Quakers published his diary, which he had dedicated to the memory of his parents and all the exiles from the coffin ships buried at sea or on that island.

His parents had loved him and that was enough. Like Ireland, he had survived and triumphed.

Conclusion:
England's Murder of the Irish

Artist Patrick Graham from Mullingar: *"Walking in certain areas in Ireland, there is an ache that is not part of consciousness. I cannot walk in certain graveyards in this country, or in some parts of the country without feeling this liquid sense of being absolutely lost. And then of anger. And this aching for a people I don't personally know, but whom I feel in my bones somehow. And that's what I paint. What I'm talking about is being born with a sense of abuse. But a sense of being abused historically."*

Britain's failure to prevent starvation in Ireland was genocide. England had her own people on the ground in Ireland telling her how bad things were, yet she still exported food from a starving country. Francis Boyle, Professor of International Law at the University of Illinois, explains: "Clearly, during the years 1845-1850, the British government pursued a policy of mass starvation in Ireland with intent to destroy in substantial part the national, ethnical, and racial group commonly known as the Irish people as such. In addition this British policy of mass starvation in Ireland clearly caused serious bodily and mental harm to members of the Irish people within the meaning of the genocide Convention Article II (b)."

Early in the Famine some British authorities recognized the terrible condition of Ireland. In a debate in the House of Lords, Prime Minister Russell asserted, "We have made it [Ireland] the most degraded and miserable country. All the world is crying shame upon us; but we are equally callous to our ignominy and to the results of our misgovernments."

After visiting Ireland, English Quaker William M. Forster echoed Russell's words. In a Report to the Central Relief Committee of Quakers in December, 1846, Forster explained: "'The hunger is upon us,' was everywhere the cry, and involuntarily we found ourselves regarding this hunger as we should an epidemic looking on starvation as a disease . . . our wonder was not that the people died, but that they lived . . . . vast numbers of our fellow countrymen have not leave to live. This is not only a national misfortune, but a national sin . . . which will be a blot in the history of our country, and make her a by-word among the nations."

Even anti-Catholic newspapers, such as *The Illustrated London News* were critical of the English government: "We have not done our duty by Ireland. Neglect, carelessness, and laissez-faire do not make a cheap system of government, but a very costly one. There is only one book the English believe in—the ledger."

In addition to those Irish who starved to death, typhus accompanied hunger, attacking those already weak and lying on the damp dirt floors of the cottages in Skibbereen. With no soap, no washing or boiling of clothes, filth accumulated from urine and excrement in the rough clothes of the Irish poor. Abrasions became hosts for the parasite. The typhus that killed the Kevanes at Grosse Ile—"ship fever"— comes from the louse, a wingless parasite which families carried with them in their clothes. The feces of the louse dry to a fine powder and spread through the air and fingertips to the victim's eyes, nostrils, and mouth feeding on the blood vessels. Like many other Irish families, the Kevanes passed the disease to each other.

Elaborating on his charge of genocide against the English, Professor Boyle writes, "During the years 1845-1850 the British government knowingly pursued a policy of mass starvation in Ireland that constituted acts of genocide against the Irish people." British officials in Ireland, the Quakers, and Irish writers emphasized to the Crown that it was starving Ireland. Writing to Lord John Russell, Lord Clarendon, Lord Lieutenant of Ireland, said of the House of Commons, "I don't think there is another legislature in Europe that would disregard such suffering as now exists in the west of Ireland, or coldly persist in a policy of extermination."

Edward Twistleton, the British head of the Poor Law Commission, resigned his post in 1849 because "many were dying or wasting away in the west of Ireland and that it is quite possible for England to prevent the occurrence of any death from starvation by the advance of a few hundred pounds." He resigned on the grounds that "the destitution here in Ireland is so horrible, and the indifference of the House of Commons to it so manifest, that I am an unfit agent of a policy that must be one of extermination."

Charles Trevelyan, in charge of Famine relief for Ireland, blamed the Irish for their fate, as if they had caused the destruction of the potato: "the deep and inveterate root [of Ireland's troubles] has been laid bare by a direct stroke of an all-wise and all-merciful providence." He writes also, "The judgement of God sent the calamity to teach the Irish a lesson, that calamity must not be too much mitigated. The real evil is not the physical evil of the Famine but the moral evil of the selfish perverse, and turbulent character of the people." The evil to which Trevelyan refers was Catholicism, the Irish not members of the Established Church. For Trevelyan the Famine was the "mechanism for reducing surplus population," in other words, genocide through starvation.

Asenath Nicholson rejected Trevelyan's view of the Famine as divinely ordained: "God is slandered, where it [the Famine] is called an unavoidable dispensation of His wise providence, to which we should all humbly bow as a chastisement which could not be avoided."

In New York during a sermon of 1847 while raising money for

Irish food, Archbishop Hughes fulminated against blaming God for Irish starvation: "They call it God's Famine. No! No! God's Famine is known by the general scarcity of food, which is its consequence. There is no general scarcity. . . . But political economy, finding Ireland too poor to buy the produce of its own labor, exported that harvest to a better market, and left the people to die of Famine. . . . Let us be careful, then, not to blaspheme Providence by calling this God's Famine."

Lord Monteagle, an Irish aristocrat and Member of Parliament from Limerick, wrote an open letter to Trevelyan in 1847: "[The Famine] is the failure of the staple food of the people. This is not our fault. The sword of conquest passed through our land but a century and a half back . . . tithes collected at the bayonet point—penal laws continued until 1829. . . . These things have destroyed our country—have degraded our people, and you English, now shrink from your own responsibilities."

The ineffectual revolt at Ballingarry in Tipperary by the Young Irelanders left two Irish dead and no police or English fatality. Yet the uprising engendered enormous hostility in England. Prime Minister Russell was incensed: "We have subscribed, worked, visited, clothed for the Irish. The only return is rebellion and calumny. Let us not grant, lend, clothe any more and see what that will do." However, James Hack Tuke of the Quaker Central Committee saw the revolt as merely a reason for English intransigence, "the means of steeling the hearts of many against the Irish." Tuke declared that if the Irish had weapons, "they would be immediately parted for food."

Many powerful English hated the Irish even though by the Act of Union in 1801 they were one country. The British had connived and bribed the Irish legislature to create the act. Samuel Johnson in 1779 warned an Irishman, "Do not unite with us. We should unite with you only to rob you." Lord Byron called the Act of Union between England and Ireland "the union of a shark with its prey." Nassau Senior, a political economist at Oxford and an advisor to the government, believed that the Famine was God's solution to the Irish problem, telling a colleague Benjamin Jowett that he feared "the Famine in Ireland would not kill more than a million people and that would be scarcely enough to do any good." Alfred Lord Tennyson, England's Poet Laureate, had another solution: "Could not anyone blow up that horrible island with dynamite and carry it off in pieces—a long way off?"

In the newspaper *The Nation*, Irish patriot and writer John Mitchel blames Britain for the hunger and death in his country, "The Almighty indeed sent the potato blight, but the English created the Famine." Mitchel explains, "England takes away every year fifteen millions' worth of our produce; and of that store English merchants send in English ships a large quantity to their colonies . . . set down as 'British produce and manufactures.' 'British produce' means Irish produce. . . . Nay, the more exact and logical statement of this matter would be, that Skibbereen starves, and raves, and dies, in order that Gibraltar and St. Helena and the rest of them, may be kept in good condition to support garrisons, and victual cruisers, and maintain the naval power of Great Britain in all the ends of the earth."

But for all the Russells, Seniors, and Trevelyans, were the Quakers who received high praise from Asenath Nicholson: "The Society of Friends did much to stay the plague and their work was carried on by volunteers who asked no reward. . . .[The Quakers] spent no time in idle commenting on the Protestant or Papist faith, the Radical, Whig, or Tory politics, but looked at things as they were and faithfully recorded what they saw. . . . they relieved, they talked and wrote but acted more. As I followed in their wake through the country the name of 'blessed William Forster' was on the lips of the poor cabiners. . . . When the question was put Who feeds you, or who sent you these clothes, the answer was 'the good quakers lady and they that have the religion entirely.'"

* * *

In 1849 the Irish lost their last and best friend when the Quakers gave up their relief work. Prime Minister Russell wished to donate 100 pounds towards any efforts the Quakers would make toward taking over all the workhouses in the west of Ireland. In his reply to Russell on 5 June 1849, Jonathan Pim spoke for the Central Relief Committee in Dublin turning down the request, explaining that the "great and prevailing distress in many parts" and the problem of relief "was far beyond the reach of private exertion, that the Government alone could raise the funds and carry out the measures necessary in many districts to save the lives of the people. The condition of our country has not improved despite the great exertion made by charitable bodies." Only strong government intervention could have improved things in Ireland. It never came.

As the American economist and historian, Joel Mokyr, writes, "Most serious of all, when the chips were down in the frightful summer of 1847, the British simply abandoned the Irish and let them perish. There is no doubt that Britain could have saved Ireland. The British treasury spent a total of about £9.5 million on Famine relief. Financed largely by advances from London, the soup kitchen program, despite its many inadequacies, saved many lives. When the last kitchen closed in October of 1847, Lord Clarendon wrote in despair to Prime Minister Russell: "Ireland cannot be left to her own resources. . . . we are not to let the people die of starvation." Russell replied, "The state of Ireland for the next few months must be one of great suffering. Unhappily, the agitation for Repeal [of the Act of Union] has contrived to destroy nearly all sympathy in this country."

Modern Irish historian Peter Gray explained that "Christian economics" proposed the laissez-faire philosophy as God's "natural economic laws," necessary for moral rectitude. According to this theory, the Famine was an act of "providentialism," a punishment levied by God on the Irish for being Catholic, the potato blight a remonstrance from the Almighty. Irish Protestants and English commentators viewed the Irish Catholics as guilty by locating "the blame for the state of Irish society squarely on the moral failings of Irish men of all classes," that is, their Catholicism.

In *The Irish Famine*, Gray points out that England spent seven million pounds for relief during 1845-1850, "representing less than half of one percent of the British gross national product over five years. Contemporaries noted the sharp contrast with the 20 million pounds [of] compensation given to West Indian slave owners in the 1830's."

Helen Hatton's *The Largest Amount of Good* points to Skibbereen as emblematic of England's policy of starvation in Ireland: "Skibbereen remains the quintessential example for those polemicists convinced of the English government's willingness to let Ireland starve. Skibbereen is the incontrovertible evidence for those who held the English government pursued a policy to allow the Famine to solve Irish problems. By so reducing the population, Ireland's quarrelsome energies would be depleted. Its reduced numbers would reduce the drain on the Treasury."

Irish historian Cormac O'Grada agrees with Nobel economist Amartya Sen that "modern Famines reflect a severe indifference on the part of the government in those countries where they occur." Sen also declares that "Famine is always a preventable occurrence if only the government in question has the will to prevent it." The English simply didn't have the will. John Waters asserts that the Famine "was an act of genocide, driven by racism and justified by ideology."

The potato blight that devastated Ireland was little understood at the time. The Greek name of the fungus is *phytopthora infestans*, "plant destroyer." Scientists think the disease originated from guano fertilizer from South America. It started in Belgium and England before reaching Ireland in the cargo holds of ships. The fungus lighted on the leaves of the potato plant, and rain washed it into the soil. Then the wind and rain blew the spores across the country at fifty miles a day. It wasn't until 1880 that a French scientist discovered a cure for the blight, a mixture of lime and copper sulphate.

By 1851 the potato destruction had essentially passed, and a devastated people were struggling to rebuild their lives. In addition to the million Irish poor who died, their saviors suffered too. William Todhunter, who was so helpful with the Quaker effort to revive fishing in Ireland, died in 1850 in Dublin of exhaustion. Joseph Bewley died in 1851, also of exhaustion. Of him, Jonathan Pim, his co-worker and friend, said, "For the sufferings of every class his heart was open to feel, and liberally but unostentatiously were his pecuniary means employed in the alleviation of distress and in contributing to increase the comforts of those whose resources were limited."

Besides the soup kitchens, the model farm, the help with Irish fisheries, the Quakers attacked the causes of poverty in Ireland, as stated by Jonathan Pim in Transactions of the Central Relief Committee of The Society of Friends: "the evils of insecurity of tenure and the existing laws of real property." Thomas P. O'Neill gave a more recent analysis of the effect the Quakers had for good. "The real merit of the activities of the Quakers, at least their greatest ultimate value, lay not in the immediate steps to alleviate distress but in the approach to the fundamental economic causes of poverty in Ireland. The number whose lives they saved will never be known, but their views on land tenure helped to mould public opinion."

John Waters describes the effect of the Famine on today's Ireland: "The Famine left an endless array of legacies which live with us to the present moment: the hemorrhaging of our youth, the corruption of our spirituality, the destruction of our independence of spirit, the final assault on our sense of the self. But it would be an even greater tragedy if that calamitous event, which carries such a shocking emblematic truth about our history, were to be used to lock us out forever from the truth of that history."

In 1997 Britain's Prime Minister Tony Blair apologized to the Irish people in a letter read at an event in County Cork to commemorate the Famine in Ireland and its subsequent effect on society and politics: "Those who governed in London at the time failed the people through standing by while a crop failure turned into a massive human tragedy. That one million people died in what was then part of the richest and most powerful nation in the world is something that still causes pain as we reflect on it today."

Today Ireland has a population of over five million people, while it is estimated there are more than seventy million people of Irish descent throughout the world.

ERIN-In forty years I have lost, through the operation of no natural law, more than Three Millions of my Sons and Daughters, and they, the Young and the Strong, leaving behind the Old and Infirm to weep and die. Where is this to end?

Source: *Supplement, Weekly Freeman, 2 July 1881.*

Selected Bibliography

Gallagher, Thomas. *Paddy's Lament.* New York: Harvest Book, 1982.

Gray, Peter. *The Irish Famine.* London: Thames and Hudson, 1995.

Hatton, Helen E. *The Largest Amount of Good.* Kingston: McGill-Queens University Press, 1993.

Irish Hunger. Hayden, Tom, Ed. Boulder, Colorado: Roberts Rinehart Publishers, 1997.

Kerr, Donal A. *A Nation of Beggars.* Oxford: Clarendon Press, 1994

Kinealy, Christine and Mac Atasney, Gerald. *The Hidden Famine.* London: Pluto Press, 2000.

Laxton, Edward. *The Famine Ships.* New York: Henry Holt, 1996.

Luddy, Maria. *Women and Philanthropy in Nineteenth-Century Ireland* (Paperback) New York: Cambridge University Press, 1995

Miller, Kerby. *Emigrants and Exiles.* Oxford: Oxford University Press, 1985.

Mokyr, Joel. *Why Ireland starved: a quantitative and analytical history of the Irish economy, 1800–1850.* New York: Taylor & Francis Group, 2006.

Nicholson, Asenath. *Lights and Shades of Ireland.* (1850). Ed. Maureen Murphy. London: Gilpin.

O Grada, Cormac. *Black '47 and Beyond.* New Jersey: Princeton University Press, 1999.

Poirtier, Cathal. *Famine Echoes.* Dublin: Gill 1995.

Quigley, Michael. "Grosse Ile: Canada's Irish Famine Memorial." *Labour/Le Travail* 39 (Spring 1997) 195-210.

Robert Whyte's Famine Ship Diary. Ed. James J. Mangan. Dublin: Mercier Press, 1994.

Scally, Robert James. *The End of Hidden Ireland.* New York: Oxford University Press, 1995.

The Great Irish Famine. Ed. Cathal Poirtier. Pennsylvania: Dufour Editions, 1995.

The Meaning of the Famine. Ed. Patrick O'Sullivan. Leicester University Press: London, 1999.

Electronic Sources

http://irelandsown.net/holocaust.html The Great Hunger: Famine or Holocaust? Máirtín Pilib de Longbhuel.

http://irelandsown.net/afroirish.html Out of Africa, Out of Ireland. James Mullin

http://www.bbc.co.uk/history/british/victorians/famine_01.shtml

http://www.nde.state.ne.us/SS/Irish/Irish_pf.html

Links to Web Resources concerning the Famine and Irish History

Irish Resources in the Humanities

Ask About Ireland - the National Digitization Project

Great Irish Famine Curriculum

The Great Hunger Foundation

IASIL - The International Organization for the Study of Irish Literatures

http://www.law.umn.edu/irishlaw/ LAWS IN IRELAND FOR THE SUPPRESSION OF POPERY commonly known as the PENAL LAWS (The University of Minnesota Law School)

General Irish & British
History Sites on the Web

http://ux1.eiu.edu/~cfnek/workshops/teacher.htm

http://www.eiu.edu/~localite/britain/

Related
(External) Web Sites

World Food Programme

Irish American Historical Society

Strokestown Park and Famine Museum, Ireland

Parks Canada - Grosse Île and the Irish Memorial National Historic Site of Canada

Questions for Book Club
Discussions of *Famine Ghost*

1. Is Johnjoe Kevane, his life and trials, an appropriate symbol for the tragedy of the Irish during The Great Famine?

2. Captain Packenham represents the hatred of the dragoons for the Irish poor. Is his death an appropriate ending to his life?

3. Major Mahon and Mr. Gray are "landgrabbers," representing all those native Irish who preyed on the poor in their own country. They used religion as the pretext for their actions. What other historical tragedies used religion for hatred?

4. Why were the Quakers, though of a different religion, so generous to Irish Catholics?

5. The clergy on the parish and school level described in the book acted on the side of the poor, yet the Catholic hierarchy in Rome and even in Ireland opposed rebellion against England. Why? Have there been other instances in the world when Catholic Church officials failed their people?

6. What did you think of Prime Minister Blair's apology to the Irish people for the Famine? Besides his words, could he have done anything more for the Irish?

7. In recent years there has been a scandal of physical and sexual abuse in Ireland committed by priests, brothers, and nuns. Consult the "Ryan Report" for details. In light of this abuse, do we look at all the good works done by the clergy during the Famine any differently? Were all those good deeds obliterated by today's revelations?